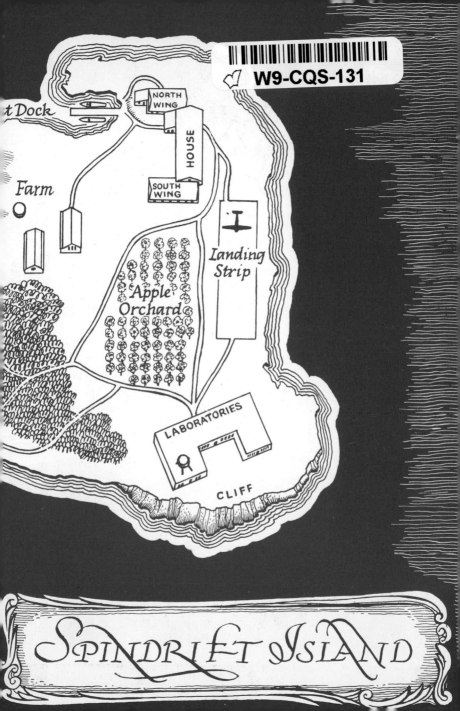

SEA GOLD

The RICK BRANT SCIENCE-ADVENTURE *Stories*

BY JOHN BLAINE

———•••———

THE ROCKET'S SHADOW
THE LOST CITY
SEA GOLD
100 FATHOMS UNDER
THE WHISPERING BOX MYSTERY
THE PHANTOM SHARK
SMUGGLERS' REEF
THE CAVES OF FEAR
STAIRWAY TO DANGER
THE GOLDEN SKULL
THE WAILING OCTOPUS
THE ELECTRONIC MIND READER
THE SCARLET LAKE MYSTERY
THE PIRATES OF SHAN
THE BLUE GHOST MYSTERY
THE EGYPTIAN CAT MYSTERY
THE FLAMING MOUNTAIN

Cunner's visitor was Fred Lewis!

SEA GOLD

By JOHN BLAINE

GROSSET & DUNLAP   PUBLISHERS

NEW YORK, N. Y.

Printed in the United States of America

Contents

CHAPTER		PAGE
I	TROUBLE AT CRAYVILLE	1
II	RICK GETS A TELEGRAM	18
III	THE SEA MINE	27
IV	PRESSURE: TEN ATMOSPHERES	41
V	WAS IT SABOTAGE?	51
VI	BARBY BAKES A CAKE	61
VII	CUNNER HAS A VISITOR	78
VIII	THE PLAYING GETS ROUGH	90
IX	THE WARNING	107
X	CUNNER'S RAID	113
XI	THE CAR WITH THE BROKEN BUMPER	129
XII	THE MANILA ENVELOPE	140
XIII	SCOTTY TAKES A HAND	148
XIV	FRED LEWIS'S SECRET	160
XV	SHADOWS IN THE NIGHT	169
XVI	SWIM—OR DIE!	172

XVII   AN ANGEL IN A LOBSTER SMACK . . 185
XVIII SETTING THE TRAP 191
XIX   THE TRAP CLOSES 200
XX   SUCCESS! 206

SEA GOLD

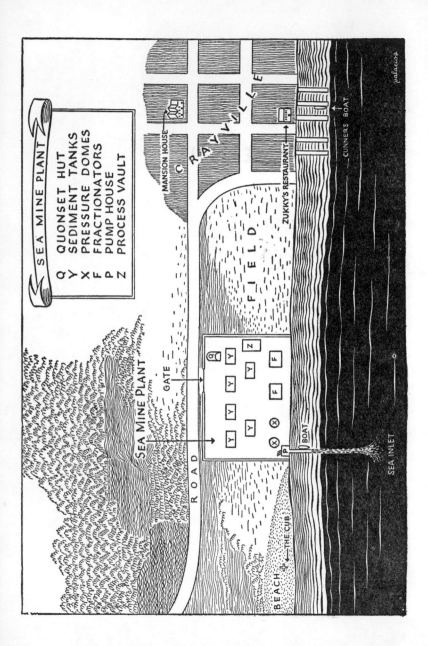

CHAPTER 1

Trouble at Crayville

THE coast of Connecticut slid by under the wing of the yellow Piper Cub. There were alternate stretches of green coastal land and sandy beaches. Now and then an attractive little town appeared and passed below. To the east, Long Island Sound glittered blue and green in the noonday sun, and Long Island itself was a low bulk on the far horizon.

Rick Brant, sitting on the passenger's side of the little plane, stretched and gave a luxurious yawn. He was a slim boy of high school age, with light brown hair and brown eyes that always had a twinkle lurking in them.

He was at peace with the world today. School had just closed and the long summer stretched pleasantly ahead. He didn't know yet how the vacation would be spent, but something would turn up.

He made a lazy check of the instrument panel and

the plane's position, then grinned at the husky, dark-haired boy who was piloting.

"Flying Chinese again " Rick accused.

Don Scott, called "Scotty," snapped out of his absorbed contemplation of something under the left wing. "Chinese? What're you talking about?"

"One Wing Low," Rick said. "Straighten up and fly right, bird-boy."

Scotty gave the control wheel a slight turn and leveled off. "Have to watch that. Every time I look out the port window the wing goes down."

Referring to left and right as "port and starboard" was a habit Scotty had brought back from his service in the Marines. Although only a year Rick Brant's senior, he had three years of wartime duty with the Marines behind him.

"What's so interesting down there?" Rick asked. He craned to see, but the fuselage blocked his vision.

"There's a funny-looking factory of some kind next to that town," Scotty said. He obligingly rocked the plane up on a wing and pulled around in a tight bank so that Rick could see.

Rick gazed down through two thousand feet of emptiness to where a small town lay against the shore. Directly south of it he saw a plot of ground on the water front that harbored what might have been two enormous beehives, half a dozen swimming pools, and miscellaneous other buildings.

He reached for the road map by which they were navigating. "Let's see . . . we've passed Bridgeport, but we haven't reached New Haven . . ." He made a quick check. "That's Crayville!"

Scotty gave him a puzzled look. "All right, it's Crayville. Why the excitement?"

"That's the new sea mine plant down there."

"It is?" Scotty looked blank.

"I saw an item about it in the paper," Rick explained. "Two men have a new process for mining the sea, and they're putting up the plant at Crayville. Boy, I'd like a closer look at it."

"I'm dense," Scotty said. "If anyone asked me what mining the sea was, I'd tell 'em it's planting mines to blow up ships."

"Not that kind." Rick grinned. "This mine extracts minerals from sea water. It's not a new idea. There are quite a few plants that extract magnesium and bromine from sea water, but the paper said these guys have some new processes that will get a lot of other stuff out of the water, too. Maybe even gold."

Scotty was looking down with new interest. "Some stunt, if they can do it."

"They probably can," Rick said. An idea had been taking form in his mind. "Listen, remember what we said yesterday about getting jobs for the summer?"

"You thinking of getting jobs down there?"

"Sure! As long as the professors haven't anything

cooking at Spindrift, we could try to get jobs on some kind of scientific project."

The professors Rick referred to were the world-famed scientists who lived on Spindrift Island and had their laboratories there. Rick's father, Hartson W. Brant, was head of the important scientific group that already had contributed so much to the science of electronics.

It was during one of the experiments, sending a controlled rocket to the moon, that Rick had met Scotty. The ex-Marine had rescued him from a possible beating at the hands of Manfred Wessel's gang, and later had been instrumental in defeating the renegade scientist's efforts to destroy the Spindrift Island rocket.

After the adventure of "The Rocket's Shadow," Scotty, who was an orphan, had become an accepted member of the Spindrift Island family. Later, the two boys had gone with Professor Hobart Zircon and Professor Julius Weiss to High Tibet, to set up a radar transmitter for sending messages via the moon. They had succeeded only after overcoming many obstacles thrown in their way by the unscrupulous adventurer, Hendrick Van Groot, and the lost tribe of Mongols whose city was hidden in the Valley of the Golden Tomb, as related in "The Lost City."

Since then, however, no experiments of an important nature had been started, and the boys, foreseeing no adventures on Spindrift Island, had discussed getting jobs for the summer.

Rick turned the idea over in his mind. His great ambition was to follow in his famous father's footsteps and become a leading electronic scientist. Mining the sea was new; it would be exciting and he could learn a great deal.

"Let's go down and look it over," he said impulsively.

"We might land on that stretch of beach, if it's packed hard enough," Scotty suggested.

In a few moments they were low over the water, running parallel with the beach.

"It looks okay," Rick said, after a survey. "Think you can put her in?"

Scotty was learning to handle the Cub surprisingly well, but he had never made a landing on anything but a good field. His eyes searched for possible obstacles.

"I think so," he answered finally.

Rick tightened his safety belt. "Okay."

The Cub banked sharply around as Scotty lined up the stretch of beach. In a moment Rick saw sand below. The beach came up with a slight jar, and then they were rolling to a stop on the hard-packed sand.

"Nice going," Rick commented. He stepped out onto the beach as Scotty cut the engine. The sea mine plant was only a few hundred yards away.

Scotty joined him and they stood looking at what they could see of it over the high board fence. There was no sound from inside.

"The place seems to be deserted," Rick said.

"It's Sunday, remember," Scotty reminded him. "They're probably sleeping as all sensible people should do on a Sunday afternoon."

Rick already was striding up the bank toward the road that led past the plant. His active imagination raced ahead of him. He had visions of great quantities of sea water pouring into the plant in a steady rush, to be reduced finally to gold, silver, magnesium, aluminum, or any one of a thousand other things. And he had a vision of himself taking part in the magic transformation of sea water to valuable minerals.

"I was wrong," Scotty remarked as they reached the road. "Look."

A man stood at what was evidently the plant gate. He seemed to be trying to peer through a crack in the boards that formed the gate.

"He must have just come from church," Rick said. "Those certainly aren't work clothes he's wearing."

The man was attired in a severe black suit, and he wore a starched collar, black string tie, and a white shirt. A gray hat was pulled down low on his forehead.

"Lucky break," Scotty said. "He's probably one of the owners coming to see whether his plant is still there."

Rick cupped his hands to his mouth. "Hello!"

The man's head jerked up in surprise. Rick caught a glimpse of a face startling even at that distance. It was astonishingly white.

"Hey! He's running!" Scotty exclaimed.

The man had turned and was departing on a dead run. He rounded a corner of the board fence and disappeared. In a moment they heard the roar of a car engine and a black sedan shot out from beyond the fence and vanished in the direction of the town. Rick just had time to notice that the car's rear bumper hung at an angle. One end of it almost touched the ground.

"Well, that beats me!" Rick exclaimed. "He took off like a P-80 as soon as he saw us."

"Maybe we startled him."

"He must have seen the Cub," Rick pointed out.

"He probably saw us when we were up high," Scotty agreed, "but this fence is pretty tall. I doubt that he saw us sit down on the beach, although he must have heard the motor."

Rick nodded. A man standing at the gate of the high fence wouldn't have been able to see them land. Perhaps he had thought the plane was just buzzing the beach. But that didn't explain why the man had run. Rick scratched his head, still bewildered.

"Do you suppose he was trying to break in?" he asked.

Scotty grinned. "If he was, he was the silliest-looking burglar I've ever seen."

Rick recalled the severe black suit and the stiff collar and laughed. "How many burglars have you seen?" he asked.

"I had a platoon full of 'em," Scotty said. "Let's see if anyone's at home."

Actually, there were two gates, Rick saw. One was normal size, cut into the fence, the other composed of two whole sections of fence that could be swung back to admit the biggest trucks. Rick applied his eye to a crack in the door but could see no sign of life.

"Nobody home," he said. "We'll have to come back tomorrow."

Scotty gave him a quizzical look. "I recognize the tone of voice. You've already sold yourself on the idea of working here."

"Why not?" Rick said, grinning sheepishly. "So what if I do make up my mind in a hurry? Proves I have a mind to make up."

"It's okay," Scotty assured him. "I've always wanted to work in a sea mine." He looked longingly in the direction of town. "What do you say we rustle up a little chow? My stomach tells me it's time to eat."

"You and that stomach," Rick jeered. "You should hire it out to the Bureau of Standards in Washington as a stand-in for their time clock."

"I'm a healthy, growing boy," Scotty said with dignity. "Can I help it if I need lots of vitamins? Come on, let's stake the plane down and set up the alarm."

They walked swiftly back to the plane and took four steel stakes and a coil of wire out of the baggage compartment. Working with the speed of long practice.

they pushed the stakes into the sand in the form of a square around the plane, then strung them with two strands of wire, forming a low fence.

Rick took the ends of the wires and led them into the plane through the door, which he left partially ajar. He connected them to clips on a black metal box. Then, careful not to touch any part of the plane, he reached through the door and flipped a switch.

This was his own adaptation of the standard electric fence, plus an automobile burglar alarm. If anyone touched the fence they would get a harmless but frightening shock. If they jumped the fence and touched the plane, a loud horn would be set off, continuing its ear-splitting blast until someone came to disconnect it.

"Come on," Scotty said impatiently. "I'll faint from weakness and you'll have to carry me." He leaped over the fence and started for the road.

Rick hastened to fall in step. Now that Scotty had mentioned it, he felt hungry, too. "I'll bet we could get jobs," he mused. "They must have a lot of electrical equipment. We could help with that."

"Sure," Scotty said. "Can't you see me with my grand-children on my knee? I'll tell 'em: 'Yep, Grampy worked in a sea mine once. I'll never forget it. You should've seen us drill the shafts. Straight down a hundred fathoms. The fish used to watch us go by, and their jaws'd be hanging open. Some of 'em worked for us. We hired sculpins to pull up the bags of gold.'"

"How did you keep the water from filling up the shafts again, grandpop?" Rick asked, in a high voice like a small boy's.

"I thought you'd ask that, son," Scotty said, stroking an imaginary beard. "We had a boy, name of Brant, working for us with a sea scoop. When the shaft'd start to fill, he'd scoop it out. He was good at it, too. Strong back and a weak mind, is why. If he'd been smart like me, he'd 'a known you can't drill holes in water, and he'd likely been drowned. It don't pay to know too much."

"You're the living proof of that," Rick said in his normal voice and ducked as Scotty swung. "Remember," he cautioned, "you're weak from needing food. Don't wear yourself out."

At the mention of food, Scotty became serious again. "That's gospel, son. Let's shake a leg." He lengthened his stride toward the little town up the road.

As they reached the outskirts, Rick looked around him, agreeably surprised. From the air, Crayville hadn't looked like much, but here, on the edge of the town, there were neat little houses, with neatly cropped, green lawns. But, as they entered the town itself, the air of well-being gave way to one of neglect. A big frame structure with a faded sign that proclaimed it *The Mansion House* dominated the central green. There were a few stores, and a dilapidated motion-picture house.

Closer to the water front, they began to see signs of the town's chief industry. Nets, lobster pots, barrels, and rusted fishing equipment. The houses had a dried, weather-beaten look, and the atmosphere was a combination of odors—salt water, tidal marshes, fishing boat engines, and fish long departed from this world.

Scotty remarked on the fact that they hadn't seen a sign of life. "I know what the principal industry is here," he added. "It isn't fishing, it's sleeping."

They reached the water front and saw that a board-walk ran along it, a sort of entryway to piers that thrust out into the water. Scotty pointed to a fifty-foot boat tied up near by. "Looks like a tug," he remarked.

"It's a dragger," Rick told him. "They tow big nets from those things. This town supplies a lot of fish—flounders mostly—to the New York markets."

Suddenly Scotty lifted his head and sniffed. Rick grinned. He always maintained that his friend could scent food farther than a bird dog could scent quail.

"Now what?"

"Clam chowder," Scotty said longingly. "It can only be clam chowder." He inspected the dock area. "Doesn't that sign say restaurant?"

"It did once," Rick agreed. "Let's give it a try." The appetizing aroma of sea food sharpened his own appetite.

As they hurried toward the door, Rick took a closer look at the sign. He was able to make out *Zukky's*

Restaurant. It was open for business, all right, and it seemed to be crowded.

"This is where the town is spending its Sunday," Scotty said. "Let's go in."

The mingled aromas of smoke, sawdust, beer, and sea food struck their noses forcibly as they pushed through the door and stepped down the two steps to floor level. Booths were lined against one wall, and the floor was crowded with tables. A number of men glanced up as the boys entered and Rick guessed that they must be fishermen. Their faces were as weather-beaten as the restaurant sign, and they wore nondescript clothes.

Towering over four other men seated around one table Rick saw a man who looked more like a lumber-jack than a fisherman. He was young and blond, with massive shoulders that stretched the fabric of a bright red shirt. The big man met Rick's eyes and grinned. At least one friendly face in the crowd, Rick thought. The expressions of the other fishermen ranged from dis-interest to scowls.

Scotty spotted a counter and swung his leg over a vacant stool. Rick took the stool next to him. The counterman came toward them and made a pretense of wiping off the counter with a much-used dish towel.

"Yeah?" His eyes swung from one to the other, and the toothpick in his mouth followed suit.

"Two clam chowders," Scotty said, not bothering to consult Rick.

"Yeah." He turned toward the kitchen, seeming to resent the need of moving.

Rick looked into the dingy mirror behind the counter and could see almost the whole restaurant. A pudgy man with a round, red face was moving from table to table, stopping to talk with the fishermen. It was so noisy that Rick couldn't hear what he was saying, but he seemed violent about it, thumping the table now and then to emphasize a point.

"They ought to rent this place out to make movies," Scotty said. "I can imagine pirates striding through the door and yelling for clam chowder."

Rick grinned. It did look like the setting for a grade B thriller. "Looks like the local hangout, all right. Say, do you suppose anyone here could tell us where to find the sea mine owners? They must live near by."

"Here comes Greasy Joe," Scotty said. "Ask him."

The counterman walked gingerly toward them, balancing two steaming bowls of chowder. He put them down, reached under the counter and brought out a handful of crackers which he dropped on the counter between them.

"I beg your pardon," Rick said. "Could you tell me where we might find the owners of the sea mine plant?"

The counterman had turned to leave, but now he swung back, glaring. "What did you say?" he demanded.

He sounded ugly. Rick ignored the tone and tried again. "Where can we find the owners of the sea mine?"

He realized all at once that the noise behind him had

ceased, replaced by an ominous silence. In the mirror, Rick saw the beefy, red-faced man moving toward the counter.

Scotty spoke into the silence. "Well? What about it?"

"What do you want with those guys?" a voice behind them demanded.

The boys turned on their stools. It was the man Rick had seen in the mirror. His close-set, pale eyes switched rapidly from one boy to the other, and his jaw was thrust forward belligerently.

"Have they been in today?" Rick asked politely.

"No!" The beefy man exploded. "They ain't been in, and they better not come in!" He turned to the men at the tables. "Right, boys?"

An ugly growl of agreement rose from the room.

"What we want to know is, what do you kids want with them?"

"Business," Scotty said shortly.

The man switched his glance to Scotty. "Oh, so you're doin' business with 'em, hey? Workin' for 'em, maybe?"

"We might be," Rick answered quietly. He took in the man's unshaven face, the dirty flannel shirt that puffed from his pants top, his sparse, unkempt hair, the bulldog thrust of his jaw, and didn't like what he saw.

"Get out," the beefy man said viciously. "You guys work for the plant, you ain't wanted here. Get out."

From long experience, Rick knew when Scotty's temper was coming to a boil. He put a hand on his friend's arm, but Scotty pushed it aside and stood up.

"You want to try putting us out?" he asked.

"Easy," Rick cautioned. "I don't know what you're so upset about, mister. We only asked a civil question."

"Ask it outside. We don't want guys who work for the plant in here. Not no more than we want the plant in town. Now get goin'."

"But what's wrong with having a sea mining plant in town?" The man's hostility aroused Rick's quick curiosity.

"You know blasted well what's wrong!" The beefy man's voice rose, as though he were addressing the whole room. "The waste from that mine will ruin us! It'll turn Crayville into a ghost town. It'll ruin the fishing grounds and poison every oyster and lobster for twenty miles!"

"But they're protected by law," Rick protested.

The man took a menacing half-step toward him. "Who you callin' a liar, young feller?"

Rick felt Scotty tense and again put a hand out, but it wasn't necessary. A newcomer suddenly had come between the beefy man and the boys.

He was small and thin, with gray hair and a weathered, wrinkled face.

"Let them alone," he said quietly. "They're only boys, Stoles."

"You keep out of this, Galt!"

The thin man must have been well over sixty-five, but

he showed no fear of the blusterer. "Run along, boys," he said. He gestured toward the door.

Rick knew authority when he heard it. He obeyed the old man without question, putting some coins on the counter and motioning to Scotty. In a moment they were out on the boardwalk.

"I don't like running out," Scotty said hotly. "Why should we let an overstuffed windbag like that push us around?"

"Relax," Rick said. "The old man knew what he was talking about. We'll get out of here. There's no point in mixing in local troubles."

"Now I know I'm going after a job in the sea mine plant," Scotty said. "No greasy character like that is going to run me out of town!"

Rick felt much the same way about it, but he only shrugged. "There's nothing we can do today, anyway. Let's get started back."

"We didn't get to eat the chowder," Scotty grumbled.

"That will leave more room for waffles when we get home."

His own temper wasn't as explosive as Scotty's, but he was just as angry deep down inside—and he was curious. For some reason, the man called Stoles was spreading lies about the sea mine. Something unpleasant was cooking in Crayville.

He felt Scotty watching him.

"What's on your mind?" his friend asked.

"I was thinking," Rick told him. "Tomorrow morning let's come back to Crayville."

Scotty breathed a sigh of relief. "You had me worried. For a while I thought you were letting blubberpuss scare you off."

"I am a little scared." Rick grinned. "But not as scared as I am curious."

CHAPTER II

Rick Gets a Telegram

BARBY BRANT, a pretty girl a year Rick's junior, looked inquiringly at her brother.

"I asked did you want another waffle," she said.

Rick looked up from his plate. "Huh? Oh, no, thanks. I'm full up."

"I'll have one," Scotty said.

"She knows that." Hartson Brant laughed. "The day Scotty refuses a waffle is the day the world ends. Or maybe the day Rick discovers perpetual motion."

Seated with his family at the Sunday night supper table, Hartson Brant might have been taken for almost anything but the famous scientist that he was. Except for the lines in his face, he might have been Rick's elder brother. He had the same leanness, the same speculative eyes, and the same alert, eager look that marked his son. And, like Rick, he preferred comfortable old clothes with open shirt collar and moccasin-style shoes.

18

Scotty accepted the waffle without comment, spread it liberally with butter, and poured on a pint of syrup.

From the end of the table, Mrs. Brant spoke up. She was a small, attractive woman with a pleasant face.

"Never mind, Scotty," she said, "don't pay any attention to them."

"He's building up his muscles," a stocky young man spoke up from across the table. "He knows there's no hope for his brains."

Scotty withered him with a glance and went on eating.

Jerry Webster, a reporter for the Whiteside, New Jersey newspaper, and a regular attendant at the Brant Sunday night waffle suppers, continued, "He'll need muscles if he takes that job I offered him."

"What job?" Instantly Barby Brant was all ears.

"He and Rick can have jobs at the paper for the summer. I asked the boss and he said it was all right."

Barby gave a delighted squeal. "Reporters? Honest, Jerry? Can you get me a job, too?"

Jerry grinned. "The jobs are as muscle men in the distribution department. They'd have to wrestle stacks of paper."

"Oh!" Barby's enthusiasm collapsed. "That's no fun." She appealed to Rick. "Is it?"

Rick had been lost in thoughts of his own. "Is what what?"

"You're in a daze," Barby accused. "You haven't heard a word."

"Clatter," Rick said airily. "Small talk. I'm a man with weighty problems. I have to think."

"I have intuition," Barby declared. "Do you know what? My intuition tells me you and Scotty had an adventure today. I bet!"

Sometimes Barby's perception startled Rick. He looked at her with surprised respect. "How did you know?"

"Well, when you left this morning, you were cheerful. And tonight you're glooming into the syrup pitcher as though it was a crystal ball or something. That's how I know."

Hartson Brant showed sudden interest. "How about it, Rick? I thought you took Scotty up the coast on a routine flight."

"It started out to be routine," Scotty put in. "I was just getting in some hours on my logbook. Then we spotted the sea mine—"

"Sea mine?" Mrs. Brant's voice was startled. "But those things are dangerous! Why, I read just the other day how some ship was blown up by a floating mine!"

"Not that kind of mine, Mom," Rick hastened to say. He told them about the day's events.

When he had finished, the others were silent for a moment. Then Jerry asked, "And you're going back after jobs?"

"If it's all right," Rick said. He gave his father a pleading glance.

"It might be interesting," Hartson Brant agreed. "I would discount what you heard in the restaurant. As you pointed out, the law protects fishing grounds from factory wastes. And, in addition, I can't imagine what wastes from a sea water processing plant could possibly be poisonous."

"But it's so far away," Mrs. Brant protested.

"Not very," Rick assured her. "It's only about an hour and a half flying time. We would be home every week end."

"And it's not as far as Tibet," Scotty said, grinning.

Mrs. Brant sighed. "I suppose not."

"I remember the story we carried about that plant," Jerry put in. "The owners are a couple of young fellows. One of them worked out the processes and the other one put up the money. Something like that. I can't remember all of it."

"Well, let's not cross bridges before we come to them," Hartson Brant advised. "The boys don't have the jobs yet."

"If you'll go out on the porch, I'll bring cake and coffee," Mrs. Brant invited.

"I'm afraid I can't stay," Jerry said regretfully. "I promised one of the boys I'd cover the night desk for him. Barby, how about running me back to the mainland?"

"All right. You'll save some cake for me, won't you, Mother?"

"If I can keep it away from Scotty."

Jerry thanked Mrs. Brant and said good-bye to the others, then he and Barby departed in the direction of the boat landing.

Spindrift Island was separated from the New Jersey mainland by a rocky tidal flat, under water at high tide. Transportation to Whiteside, the nearest town, was by motorboat, or by Rick's Cub. Two fast motorboats were kept in a hook-shaped cove below the big house, which was located on the north side of the island, overlooking the sea.

Hartson Brant and the two boys went out to the big screened porch as Jerry and Barby left. Rick walked to the end of the porch and looked across the edge of the orchard to where the gray bulk of the laboratories dominated the south tip of the island. It seemed strange not to see the building ablaze with light.

"I wonder what the professors are doing now," he said. "I'll bet they miss Spindrift."

"So their letters say," Hartson Brant said. "But they're all very busy. Hobart has something up his sleeve that I think we may hear about soon."

He referred to Hobart Zircon, the big, bluff scientist who had been with the expedition to Tibet. He was in Washington now, studying at the Institute of Oceanography. Julius Weiss, the little mathematician, was also in Washington. The other two professors, Dr. Wisecarver and Professor Gordon, were out on the Pacific coast.

Thinking of Hobart Zircon and Tibet brought to mind the newest member of the Spindrift Island family. Chahda, the Hindu boy who had become their friend and ally on the Tibetan expedition, was at school in Massachusetts, studying hard. He had refused to take the summer vacation, preferring to take special courses.

"This way," he had written, "I think so I get smart two times as fast. But I come home in maybe August. This school has much more fact than my *World Almanac*."

Chahda's education had been a great source of amusement to the boys. He had laboriously memorized most of a very old edition of *The World Almanac*.

"I feel sort of guilty about not being at home with everyone else away," Rick said.

Hartson Brant smiled. "Don't feel too guilty," he said. "There wouldn't be much excitement for you here."

Rick returned the smile gratefully. He had the best parents in the world, he thought. They encouraged his ideas—whether they took the form of going to Connecticut to work for the summer, or whether they were perfectly useless inventions such as he sometimes turned out.

A sharp bark sounded from the direction of the

orchard. Rick whistled and a shaggy little dog came trotting over. He scratched at the screen door and was admitted.

At once Hartson Brant and Scotty let out sharp protests. A harsh, distinctive odor smote Rick's nose forcibly. "Dismal," he groaned.

Dismal rolled over, all four legs in the air, and played dead.

"You should," Rick said sternly. "Will you ever learn to keep away from skunks?"

Dismal whined for forgiveness.

"Outside," Rick ordered.

"Wait until Barby comes back," Hartson Brant said. "She can sprinkle him with cologne."

"It'll take more than foo-foo water to kill that smell," Scotty commented.

Mrs. Brant appeared with a loaded tray. She sniffed the air, then exclaimed, "Dismal! Not again!"

"He'll never learn," Rick said.

Dismal sat up and begged, then played dead again.

"Teach him to vanish," Scotty suggested.

As Rick led the reluctant pup outside, he heard the phone ring. Scotty ran to answer, and he heard snatches of the conversation.

"Who is it for? Just a sec . . . okay, read it . . ."

In a moment he returned, his forehead creased in a frown.

"What is it?" Hartson Brant asked.

"For Rick," Scotty said. He handed over a sheet of paper. "A telegram."

Rick read it aloud.

Mr. Galt informed me of your visit to Crayville today. He took number of your plane and learned your name from Civil Air Authority. Appreciate your interest but regret all positions at the mine are filled.

It was signed *Douglas Chambers, Crayville Sea Mine.*

"Well, how do you like that!" Scotty exclaimed.

Rick read it over again, rapidly.

"I don't," he said slowly. "Listen, how old would you say Mr. Galt was?"

"About seventy."

"And he read the license number of the Cub? When? He couldn't have seen it, except when we were over the town at two thousand feet. And could he read it that high in the air?"

"What do you mean, Rick?" Hartson Brant asked.

"It's wacky!" Rick's mind was racing. There was something else about the note that didn't ring true. After a moment's thought he got it.

"It's Sunday! There wouldn't be anyone at the Civil Air Authority office on Sunday. And listen! This is addressed to Rick Brant. Rick, not Richard. But it's Richard on my plane registration."

"A phony!" Scotty exclaimed.

"I'd say someone doesn't want you to apply for a job at the Crayville plant," Hartson Brant said.

"But who?" Rick asked. "No one up there knows us. No one could have known my nickname."

"Someone did," Scotty said flatly.

Rick looked thoughtfully into the puzzled faces around him. "Yes," he agreed. "Someone did."

CHAPTER III

The Sea Mine

SCOTTY thrust his head into Rick's room. "You about ready?"

"Almost," Rick said.

Rick's room adjoined Scotty's, but where Scotty's room brought to mind the neat efficiency of a Marine squad room, Rick's was reminiscent of a laboratory.

Along one wall ran a wide shelf containing various tools and jars of electrical parts. What appeared to be partially dismantled radio sets were here and there about the room. But the intricate unit wired to an ancient alarm clock that rested by the window, for instance, was a device that automatically lowered the window and turned on the radiator during cold weather.

The old leather armchair that seemed to be a repository for junk actually was wired so that Rick could turn on his radio, choose his station, adjust his reading lamp, cook a hamburger, whip up a milk shake, or answer the phone, all without moving more than a hand, or perhaps both hands.

Rick took a last look around to be sure he had packed all he needed, then snapped his suitcase shut. They had already had breakfast and had said good-bye to the family. It was understood that if they got jobs they would telegraph, and the family would not expect them home until the following week end.

Mrs. Brant had been upset about the mysterious telegram, but it was typical of Hartson Brant that he had been as curious as the boys about its origin. Instead of using the message as a reason for forbidding them to go to Crayville, he had contented himself with a warning, and a request that they let him know if they discovered the sender. Then he had lent them enough money to last until they got their first pay checks—if they were hired.

As they went down the back stairs and across the orchard to the Cub, Rick spoke his thoughts aloud.

"I wonder what we're walking into. I'm still in a fog about that telegram last night. It's a dead cinch that this Douglas Chambers didn't send it, because he doesn't know me from beans and neither does Mr. Galt. So who did? No one else saw us, except the men in the restaurant, and they didn't look smart enough to write their names, much less send phony telegrams."

"How about that character at the plant gate?"

"I thought of him," Rick admitted, "but I know I've

never seen him before. I couldn't forget a face like that. It looked like something carved out of Ivory soap."

"We'll find out," Scotty prophesied. "Let's get there, huh?"

"Okay," Rick said. "You fly. A few more hours in your logbook and you'll be able to get a license."

"Dismal has a license." Scotty grinned. "And he didn't have to learn to fly to get it, either."

"He'd better stop taking so much license with skunks," Rick retorted. "I don't know which is worse, skunk fumes or your gags!"

"Those jokes were good enough for my father and grandfather," Scotty replied with dignity. "They're good enough for me."

"Moss and all," Rick said. "Get in, fly-boy. I'll spin the prop for you."

In a short while the rough oval of Spindrift Island fell away below them and they headed north along the New Jersey coast.

"Head wind this morning," Rick said. "It'll take us awhile to get there."

True to his prediction, it was almost two hours before Crayville came up on the horizon. The town sparkled in the morning sunlight as they banked over it, heading for the packed strip of beach. It looked very pretty from the air.

Rick took a closer look at the sea mine plant. It was a rectangle, the long sides formed by the water front and the road. Within the rectangle, which was outlined, except on the water, by a high board fence, the various buildings were roughly arranged like the ten-spot in a pack of cards, laid on its side.

The upper row of four and the center row of two were the tanks they had noticed yesterday. On closer look, they seemed to be lined with silver, but it was probably nickel or chrome plating. On the lower side of the imaginary ten-spot, fronting on the sea, was another row of four units. The two on the left were the domes, the two on the right were square, concrete buildings.

And to carry out the playing card picture completely, in the upper right-hand corner was a Quonset hut, right where the numeral 10 would be. In the lower left-hand corner was a small concrete and wooden structure, and a small pier that extended into the water. A motorboat was tied to the pier.

Spoiling the symmetry of the ten-spot design was a solitary building, also of concrete, that nestled against the high board fence on the right-hand side.

The only other important feature was a huge conduit of some sort that extended out into the sea from the concrete and wood building in the lower left-hand corner.

The strip of beach on which they had landed was to the left of the plant, about two hundred yards from the sea mine fence.

Scotty made a smooth landing on the beach and the boys got out.

"We can leave the plane right here," Rick said. "The tide doesn't come up this high." He pointed to the line of seaweed, driftwood, and other flotsam that indicated the high water mark.

"We'd better drag up a couple of logs and tie it down, though," Scotty suggested. "There's some driftwood that will do."

They went to work, pulling the driftwood into place and tying the plane to the logs.

"We'll have to find an airport where we can refuel," Rick said. "Let's do that this afternoon."

"You talk as though we already had the jobs." Scotty grinned. He reached in behind the plane seats and brought out the electric alarm.

"They'll hire us," Rick said confidently as they planted the stakes and strung the alarm wire.

As they started for the road, Rick asked, "Are you nervous?"

"Who, me?" Scotty retorted, and then, surprisingly said, "Yes."

"Try to look intelligent," Rick advised, laughing.

They reached the road and walked along by the high board fence toward the gate. They could see that the sea mine plant gate was open, and quickened their stride.

"I'll tell 'em how to drill holes in water." Scotty grinned. "That should convince 'em."

They paused at the gate, looking in curiously. There didn't seem to be much activity. Then Rick saw the

Quonset hut, smoke issuing from a length of pipe in the roof.

"Let's try there," he suggested.

They walked in through the gate, and Scotty pointed to two young men who were talking at the opposite end of the hut.

"Looks like our people."

Rick sized them up and decided that he liked what he saw. They were about his own height, and quite young. Somewhere in their early twenties, he guessed. One had dark hair and wore glasses. He was dressed in khaki shorts. The other was blond and wore whipcord breeches. He was smoking a pipe almost as big as a closed fist.

"Good morning," Rick said when they reached the two young men. "We're looking for Mr. Chambers."

"I'm Chambers," the dark-haired man replied, "and this is my partner, Tom Blakely." He indicated the blond man in the whipcord breeches.

Rick introduced himself and Scotty, and they shook hands all around. The partners seemed to be good fellows. Rick took the telegram message from his pocket and handed it to Douglas Chambers.

"This is a wire that was telephoned to me. Did you send it, by any chance, sir?"

Chambers read it and his eyebrows went up. "No." He handed it to Tom Blakely. "What's the story?"

Rick rapidly outlined yesterday's events, and Chambers's puzzled look deepened. "I can't imagine who sent the telegram," he said. "As for the man you saw at the gate, he probably was just curious about what was inside, but I don't know why he should have run away."

"So you boys want to work here?" Tom Blakely asked.

"We're pretty handy with tools," Rick replied. "We might be able to make ourselves useful."

"Is that your plane that just buzzed us?"

"Yes."

"Couple of junior birdmen, Doug. Let's hire them. Having our hired hands come to work in a mechanized kite will give the place class."

Rick looked sharply at Blakely and met a pair of twinkling eyes. He grinned back.

Then Tom Blakely's glance went to Scotty, inspected him carefully and came to rest on the honorable discharge pin in his jacket lapel.

"What service?" asked Tom.

"Marines, sir," Scotty replied.

"An ex-Marine, as I hope to grow old quietly! I always felt kindly toward those seagoing bellhops. Junior Seabees, we used to call 'em."

Scotty's eyes were on the button in Tom's lapel. "We always used to say, 'Never hit a poor old Seabee. He might have a son in the Marines!' "

"Those two have made friends," Douglas Chambers

said to Rick dryly. "Come into our humble parlor, fellows, and we'll sign the deal."

The interior of the Quonset hut was set up as a combination office, bedroom, and kitchen. Coffee was perking on an oil stove, and the place had a rough but homelike air.

"Do you live here?" Rick asked in amazement.

"For the time being," Chambers answered. "You must have come yesterday while we were off getting a decent meal in New Haven. Tom is a worse cook than I am, and I'm terrible."

"Amen," Tom said. He winked at Rick. "I only give him heartburn, but he gives me acute frammus of the slabenglaben. Incidentally, where do you boys come from?"

"Spindrift Island," Scotty answered. "That's in New Jersey, just south of . . ."

"I know where it is," Chambers said quickly. He looked at Rick. "You said your name was Brant. And you come from Spindrift. That makes you some relative of Hartson Brant's."

"He's my father," Rick said.

"Someday," Chambers said, "I want to meet your father. Do you ever help out in the lab? I mean, can you handle a soldering iron and stuff like that?"

"Dad lets me help with the wiring."

"Swell!" Chambers gave the kitchen table a resounding smack. "That takes a big headache off my shoulders.

Tom, here, doesn't know a triode tube from a Tripoli pirate. I've been needing someone to help me with wiring."

"What can I do," Scotty asked.

"Can you keep books?" Tom queried.

Scotty shook his head.

"No help from me," Tom sighed, then explained: "Doug is the technical brains. I'm just the hired hand who keeps the books. Anyway, we'll find plenty for you to do, Scotty. Can you run a motorboat? Drive a truck? Swing a shovel?"

"Yes to all except the shovel." Scotty grinned. "I'm not very good at complicated tools."

"You're not operating yet?" Rick commented. It was more statement than question.

"We will be," Tom replied, "in about two weeks, if all goes well."

"If," Doug echoed. "There are a lot of ifs. Workmen, for one thing. We've found it harder and harder to get Crayville people to work for us. Now we know why, thanks to your visit yesterday. Of course it's a lot of hoopla about poisoning the fish. We won't have any poisonous wastes."

A shadow blocked the doorway. Rick looked up to see a dark-complexioned man staring at him and Scotty. The newcomer was of medium build, with a look of hardness about him. He had a tight mouth and piercing black eyes.

"Oh, Tony," Doug said. "Come in and meet our two new men, Rick Brant and Don Scott. Boys, this is Tony Larzo, our foreman."

"How do," Tony said shortly. He had an odd habit of squinting when he talked, and Rick got the impression that he wasn't particularly pleased to see them. But perhaps he just had a sour disposition.

"You'll want to get squared away before you go to work," Tom Blakely remarked. "If you're in need of a place to live, I can recommend the Mansion House."

"We'll try it," Rick nodded.

"Come back this afternoon and look the plant over. You can start on the payroll in the morning. As for salary . . ." Doug named a figure that suited the boys perfectly. They shook hands all around, then hiked back to the Cub.

"We're in," Scotty exulted. "Easy as pie!"

"I like both of them," Rick said. "We should have a lot of fun working here."

"Unless whoever doesn't want us around decides to make things tough."

That had been at the back of Rick's mind, too. "Check," he said. "But let's not borrow trouble."

In a little while they were pushing open the door of the Mansion House, bags in hand. They stepped into a clean but threadbare lobby, in which the principal decorations seemed to be sea shells.

"I hope the beds are more modern than that," Scotty said, pointing to a stiff ladder-back chair.

Rick did not hear him. He was staring at the clerk's desk. Standing behind the desk was the old man who had come to their rescue, Mr. Galt!

"So you weren't scared away after all," he greeted them cordially.

"No, sir," Rick said and added, "We didn't have a chance to thank you yesterday."

"My pleasure," Mr. Galt said. "I never did care much for Cunner Stoles. What can I do for you lads?"

"We'd like a room, sir."

"Call me Cap'n, lad. Cap'n Ben Galt, it used to be." He pointed to a painting of a square-rigged ship that hung behind him. "Cap'n of the *Connie B*, best sealer ever left the port o' Crayville, if I do say it who shouldn't."

The boys inspected the painting, then looked at Cap'n Galt with new respect.

"A sealer?" Rick asked.

"Aye." The old man sighed and ran a hand through his sparse gray hair. "Them was the days, lads. Crayville was a town then, I'll tell you! Sealers and whalers comin' and goin', outbound for the antarctic or the Far Pacific, or headin' up the channel with full loads of skins or oil. Times sure has changed."

"How do you happen to be working here, sir?" Scotty asked.

Cap'n Galt's surprisingly youthful eyes twinkled. "This here hotel is the curse of the Galts. I own it." He turned to his desk and riffled through some filing cards.

"Just seein' if I have a room for you." In a moment he turned back. "Course I have. I always go through the motions just to make it look businesslike."

He took a key and led the way to the stairs, talking over his shoulder. "I take it you young'uns are goin' to work at the plant. Reckon you'll like it?"

"Yes, sir." Rick hesitated. "What was all that business at the restaurant yesterday?"

"That was Cunner Stoles soundin' off. He always was a sea lawyer. Now he's takin' it on himself to make trouble for the sea mine."

"Why?" Rick asked quickly.

"Sheer meanness is my guess. One thing's sure: He don't care a hoot for the fishin' grounds. If Cunner ever did a day's honest trawlin' in his life I ain't heard of it."

"Cunner," Scotty repeated. "That's an odd name."

"His nickname. A cunner is a kind of nuisance fish that steals bait. It suits him."

They had reached the second floor and Cap'n Galt opened the door into a room at the rear of the hotel. Rick looked around, pleased. It was spacious, with twin beds, and it was very clean. Scotty was already testing the mattresses.

"Guess you'll be comfortable. The restaurant is right downstairs. Not fancy, but good. The vittles'll stick to your ribs."

Rick found the crumpled telegraph message in his pocket, smoothed it out and handed it to the old man.

"There's something we've wondered about, Cap'n. Would you know anything about this?"

Mr. Galt produced steel-rimmed spectacles and read the note through. Then he shook his head emphatically. "News to me. Who do you think sent this?"

"Cunner Stoles?" Scotty suggested.

"Not likely. He ain't got that much imagination. Can't guess who it might be. Shucks, I didn't even know you came in a airyplane."

When Cap'n Galt had gone, the boys unpacked and stowed their clothes in the ample closets. Then Rick sat down on the bed and grinned at Scotty.

"Well," he said, "we're in it. For better or worse."

Scotty nodded. "I hope we don't regret it."

"We won't," Rick assured him. "Listen, there must be some way to check up on that telegram." He went to the old-fashioned telephone on a corner table and picked it up.

"Cap'n Galt," he said, when the old man answered, "where is the Western Union office in town?"

"Ain't none," was the crisp reply. "Nearest is Milford. You want to send a telegram, you have to phone. Want me to connect you?"

"Please," Rick said.

When the Milford Western Union office answered, Rick dictated a wire to Spindrift Island, telling the Brants the good news about the jobs. Then he asked the clerk:

"Can you give me some information on a telegram sent to that address last night? It was signed by Mr. Douglas Chambers."

The clerk told him to hold the wire, but it was only a moment before Rick got the answer he expected.

"Well," Scotty prompted as he hung up, "what's the dope?"

"It was telephoned in, from Crayville," Rick replied.

"No help." Scotty shrugged. "We don't know any more now than we did before."

"Which is nothing," Rick said, "except that someone would rather not have us around."

CHAPTER IV

Pressure: Ten Atmospheres

RICK BRANT turned over on his back and a ray of early morning sunlight lanced into his eyes. He awoke, blinking, and turned away from the light. In the bed next to him he saw Scotty, a sleeping cocoon wound in a sheet. The alarm clock on the bureau told him it was half past six.

Today would be their first full day of work at the sea mine. Again he felt the stir of excitement. Yesterday's tour of the plant with Doug Chambers had fired his enthusiasm. Already he was eager to pitch in. He wanted to see salt water pouring in through the sea inlet, to be reduced ultimately to valuable minerals.

He had met an old friend yesterday, too. The Cub needed gas and oil, and their first step after lunch had been to find a near-by airport. He knew there was one near Milford, although he had never landed there. He and Scotty took off and headed inland, and in a few moments the parallel concrete ribbons of the Merritt Parkway, the great express highway from New Haven to New York, unrolled below them. A mile away from the parkway, on the seaward side, they found the airport and landed—to discover that it was run by Steve Hollis, who had taught Rick to fly when he was an instructor for the Civil Air Authority program. It had been fun, talking over old times, and Steve had invited him to drop over any time and get in a few hours flying in the beautiful Fairchild four-seater biplane that was the airport's special pride.

Then, with everything "squared away," as Scotty put it, they returned to the plant. Doug Chambers, the serious young engineer, took them on an inspection tour, pridefully showing them his brain child.

The sea mine started some distance out at sea, with a bell-shaped pipe opening six feet in diameter. From the "sea inlet," as it was called, a four-foot pipe ran back to the pump house.

From the pump, the water ran through a maze of pipes to the several places where the processing was done. There were three clearly defined processes. One was electrolysis, to be done in the square concrete buildings called fractionators.

The second process, called "destructive distillation," was done in the two concrete domes. The third part was chemical treatment. Addition of chemicals to the treated water in the tanks would precipitate certain products.

The tanks, each thirty feet long, fifteen wide and ten feet high, were set above ground on platforms of concrete blocks. They were out in the open at present, but later sheds would be built over them.

But the heart of the plant was a guarded secret. It was the building of concrete set off by itself. It was locked in the same manner as a bank vault. Within the building was the nucleus of Doug's process. Only Doug knew what was in there. Tom had been told, of course, but in his whimsical way he had said: "It's too complicated for a simple soul like me to understand. Shucks, I can't even figure out the chemistry of a cup of coffee."

Rick gathered that Tom was the business end. He had put his own money into the plant and had scouted up more. With Doug's technical brains and Tom's business ability, they had started on a shoestring.

They were completely different. Doug was dark, serious, and all business. Tom was blond, carefree, and perpetually smiling. But both of them were fighters. Rick saw that at once. They'd make a go of the plant or else!

A fly buzzed in through the open bedroom window, did a half loop and landed on a lighting fixture. Rick watched it sleepily, and thought about the man with the strangely white face they had seen at the gate on Sunday.

They had seen him again, last night. When they came into the hotel to go to bed, he was in the lobby, reading a letter. It was the first time Rick had gotten a good look

at his face. The impression of startling whiteness hadn't
been wrong. The man's face had no color in it; the skin
was like parchment, thinly stretched over the bones of
his face. And from it, two dark eyes blazed at him.

Rick and Scotty stopped short. The man glanced up,
his lips moved soundlessly, then he jumped to his feet
and walked swiftly toward the stairs, dropping an envelope. Rick picked it up, the names on it half register-
ing, and hurried after him.

"You dropped this, sir."

The man whirled, snatched the envelope, and for an
instant his eyes locked, almost fearfully it seemed, with
Rick's. Then he ran up the stairs.

The name on the envelope had been Fred Lewis.
Cap'n Galt confirmed the identification. "Says he's a
writer. Been here 'bout a month, I'd say. Strange cuss.
Ever see a face like that before? Looks like someone
skinned him."

That was a good description, Rick thought. He
wished they knew more about the white-faced man.

Rick stretched and threw the covers aside. An expertly aimed pillow caught Scotty on the side of the
head.

"Hit the deck," Rick called. "Rise and shine. It's time
to go to work."

"Tell 'em I quit," Scotty said comfortably. He started
to roll over again.

"Not on your life," Rick said. He grabbed the covers

and tugged. Scotty struggled for a moment, then gave up.

An hour later, dressed and with a hearty breakfast under their belts, they walked into the Quonset hut. Doug greeted them with a wave of his coffee cup.

"Morning. All ready for work?"

"Ready and eager," Rick answered.

Scotty looked around the hut. "Where's Tom?"

"Gone to Bridgeport. He's going to see some employment agencies and try to hire workers. We've given up trying to get Crayville people to come to work."

"Thanks to Cunner Stoles," Rick murmured.

"I'm afraid so. Tom suggested that we have some handbills printed, telling the truth about the plant, that it won't poison fish, and so on. We'll have them distributed and see if we can't overcome some of this ridiculous prejudice. But meanwhile, we need workmen."

"That will cost a lot, bringing them from Bridgeport," Rick commented.

Doug's lips tightened. "Too much. But there's nothing else we can do. Rick, you can help me finish wiring the electronic controls for the pressure domes. I want to test them this afternoon. Scotty, you said that you can drive a powerboat. I want you to help Tony. Go out to the sea inlet and check the filter screen."

The morning passed rapidly while they worked on the intricate control panel. Rick watched Doug with respect. He knew what he was doing, all right! The automatic electronic controls controlled both heat and pressure within the concrete domes. They were very complex.

Once he crawled in through the turretlike door of one of them to check a thermostat and saw that the interior was like that of an igloo, but coated with something thick, hard, and glossy.

When he asked about it, Doug answered: "That's something I dreamed up. It's plastic. We applied it while hot, and it hardened into a firm coating that's not only chemical-proof, but adds strength to the domes. They'll have to take a lot of pressure. More than ten atmospheres."

Rick thought that over. He recalled that one atmosphere was fourteen and seven-tenths pounds to the square inch. That was normal pressure at sea level. And ten atmospheres . . . one hundred and forty-seven pounds to the square inch!

When Scotty returned with the dark, wiry foreman, he stopped to say a word to Rick before trotting off to clean out one of the big sediment tanks. "Not a hard job, but this Tony is a queer cuss. No more sociable than a wild bull."

By lunchtime, the last wire had been soldered into place. Doug straightened up with a relieved sigh. "There she is. You're a neat workman, Rick. You'll be a lot of help. Well, let's have lunch, then we'll give this thing a test."

Rick, pleased at Doug's praise, took the opportunity to ask questions. "What do you expect to get out of the sea water? And how do you do it? Golly, I never saw such complex electronic circuits. Even Dad would have to think about it for a while before he could figure them out."

"I doubt that." Doug smiled. "Don't forget that your dad probably knows more about electronics than any man living. But to answer your questions, we expect to get metals, largely. There's a lot of treasure in the sea, you know. For instance, if we could get all the gold, silver, and platinum out of a single cubic mile of sea water we could build a plant ten times the size of this one and have money left over."

Rick whistled. "Are you going after gold and silver?"

"Yes, to some extent. Our main interest will be in aluminum, magnesium, and copper, but we hope to extract enough precious metals to pay for a large part of our operating cost."

"But how do you do it? I understand about electrolysis and stuff like that, but I still can't figure out how you'll get metals."

Doug laughed. "I'll tell you in detail the day you graduate from college. I'm afraid it's a little complex."

"But give me an idea of how it works," Rick persisted.

Doug scratched his head. "I don't know how to put it in simple terms. The metals we want are in solution.

That is, they're dissolved in the sea water, not in pure form, but in compounds, like copper sulphate and gold chloride. Well, I've had to figure out the electronic structure of the compound molecules, and I've made up a table of what I call molecular electronic coefficients . . ."

"Never mind," Rick said, laughing. "My head aches already. I guess I'd just better keep my eyes open and see what I can see."

"Good idea." Doug grinned. "And I'll try to explain as we go along."

The boys had intended hiking into town for lunch, but Doug invited them to share his simple meal of canned soup, crackers, and milk. Tony ate with them, sipping his soup noisily and saying nothing.

"His voice is baritone," Scotty said later, "but he drinks soup in a tenor key."

They ate hastily, anxious to get back to testing the domes. Doug told Tony to turn on the pump and suggested that the boys go along to see how it was done while he rechecked the pressure data. He would join them at the dome.

As they left Doug and walked toward the pump house, Rick tried to engage Tony in conversation.

"Have you been in the construction business long?"

"Yeah," Tony said shortly.

"Around here?" Rick persisted.

"No."

Rick gave up and they walked in silence the rest of the way.

The pump house, a large wooden shed, contained a gasoline engine geared to a large rotary pump. The big sea inlet pipe ran in one side, and smaller pipes ran out the other. Tony opened the valves leading to the pressure domes.

Scotty found the engine starter and the switch, and tried to get the engine going, without success.

"Choke it a little," Rick suggested, pointing to the choke wire.

"No," Tony growled. "Like this, see?" He put his whole hand over the carburetor air inlet, closing it off, then he pushed the starter button. The engine whirred into life. "Choke don't work," he said briefly. He shifted the gear that threw power into the pump and they heard the blades turn inside the circular housing. In a moment they could hear water gurgling.

"Let's go," Rick said.

He and Scotty hurried to the domes, leaving Tony at the pump house. Doug was standing by the domes, and the boys joined him. Out at the sea inlet, the waters of Long Island Sound gurgled and swirled. Doug made a final check on the circular door of pressure dome one, then walked back to where the boys were watching the instruments.

There was the sound of roaring water, audible even through the thick concrete. For a long while the needle of the pressure gauge remained still, then with agonizing slowness it began to climb.

"Two atmospheres," Doug said. His voice sounded loud.

The dome was full, and pressure was building. Already the mysterious processes that Rick only dimly understood were starting to take place. He watched the pressure gauge, waiting. He couldn't have said why he was so tense.

Scotty shifted from one foot to the other.

"Five atmospheres," Doug said.

They fell silent; even the gurgling of water had ceased. Only the thrum of the pump engine broke the silence.

"Eight," Doug said.

The needle quivered, advanced a half point. If they were in the dome now, pressure would crush them. What was happening to the sea water?

"Nine."

The needle crept ahead. Nine and a . . .

A tremendous gust of pressure blew Rick back, sent him tumbling head over heels. Something smashed into his ribs, driving the air out of him. He collapsed in a heap, gasping for breath. Pain ran up his left arm. Through blurred eyes he saw Scotty stagger, saw Doug hurtling back, driven by inexorable force.

Concrete rained around him.

The dome had exploded!

CHAPTER V

Was It Sabotage?

To Rick's shocked mind it seemed that broken bits of concrete rained around him for long minutes. Small pieces struck him, but fortunately no sizable chunks fell near.

For a moment he lay still, then he got to his feet, and was surprised that he still had the power of movement. A few yards away, Scotty was also getting to his feet, shaking his head dizzily. Doug Chambers put both hands on his chest and groaned.

"What happened? What happened?" Tony yelled as he ran toward them.

Rick didn't bother to answer. He called to Scotty, "Are you hurt?"

"I'm all right, but let's see how Doug is."

The ex-Marine was already kneeling at Doug's side. Rick joined him, shaking his head to clear the cobwebs from it. As the two boys bent over him anxiously, the young engineer managed a tight grin.

"I'm okay. Just had the wind knocked out of me. You all right?"

They helped him to his feet and he took a deep shuddering breath, placing a hand on his chest again. "A piece hit me, I think."

"Let's get to the hut," Rick said. "You might have a broken rib."

"Who's bleeding?" Tony asked suddenly, and then exclaimed, "Brant! Your sleeve's bloody."

Rick looked at his arm. There was a tear in the shirt sleeve, and it was wet with blood. He wondered why he hadn't felt anything.

"Come on," Scotty said.

He took Rick's good arm and led him toward the Quonset hut. Tony gave Doug Chambers a hand.

A quick examination showed that the cut wasn't serious. Scotty cleaned and bandaged it expertly, using the first-aid kit the partners kept in the hut. Doug, meanwhile, shed his shirt, disclosing an area right over his breastbone where the skin was already turning purple. He pressed gingerly, his fingers probing for a possible fracture.

"Nothing serious," he announced. "Just a bad bruise."

"You got off easy," Tony said.

"Easy is right!" Doug's lips thinned. "We might have been killed, all of us. Where were you, Tony?"

"Down by the pump house. I was checking on the water flow. Then I heard the explosion and I ran."

Rick tried to get up from the chair in which Scotty had seated him and found that his knees were shaky. He was sweating profusely. So were the others.

"Stay put," Scotty advised. "You'll be all right in a minute."

"Tony, you're all right," Doug said. "Go out, will you? Try to find out why the dome blew. And bring a piece of that concrete in here. I can't understand it," the engineer added slowly. "I know I figured the stresses right. I rechecked the specifications a dozen times. Those domes were designed to take up to fifteen atmospheres."

Rick started to comment, but the expression on Doug's face stopped him.

"It's been this way from the very beginning," Doug continued. "We knew it was risky, trying to get a plant like this going on shoestring finances, but we were sure we could do it. We planned to start on a small scale. We were going to put all the profits right back into expansion, until we had something really big. But right from the very first we had bad luck."

Rick saw an expression of sympathy forming on Scotty's lips and motioned him to be quiet. Doug felt like talking; he had to get it off his chest.

"First it was the property. A firm in New York claimed it belonged to an estate they handled. It took a lot of money for lawyer's fees before we proved we had clear title to it. Then a cable broke while we were putting the sea inlet pipe sections together, and some of the sections dropped into the mud at the bottom. It took us a week to get them out and back together again.

"Then the sediment tanks arrived. They were in sheet sections, of course. I'd ordered them specially made, with an electroplating of chrome alloy. Well, when they arrived, some of the chrome had been ground right off. The railroad compensated us for the expense of having them repaired, but we lost more time. And time means money.

"About then, the Crayville people began quitting. We tried to reason with them, but they wouldn't listen. Tom even went to a few homes and tried to talk with them, but they're not interested. A few said something about ruining the fishing, but we didn't take it too seriously— until now."

Tony came in, holding a piece of concrete.

"And now this," Doug finished. "It cost us plenty to have those domes built. I can't understand . . . oh, Tony. Let's see that."

He took the piece of concrete and examined it. The boys went to his side and watched.

"The side blew out," Tony said.

Doug crumbled a piece of the concrete and rolled it between his fingers. "That's funny," he said as it crumbled, "it shouldn't do that."

He found a wrench and struck the concrete a sharp blow. It fell to pieces in his hand.

"Well, now we know," he said. He sounded very tired. "This stuff isn't much stronger than so much sand. The plastic seal evidently held in the pressure until it finally gave. The concrete just wasn't strong enough."

"Someone doped off," Scotty said.

"So it seems," Doug said grimly. He took the shattered concrete to the door and examined it in the bright sunlight. Then, suddenly, he held it close to his eyes, rubbing it with his finger. "That's strange," he mused. "I wonder where this white powder came from."

Rick looked over his shoulder and saw flecks of white mixed in with the gray. "Maybe it's raw cement," he suggested.

"No. All the cement would have combined in the mixture. This is something else."

Doug dumped the stuff on the table, then went to a cabinet, opened it, and brought out a case from which he took a microscope. He explained as he plugged in the cord that lit the small bulb at the bottom: "I have this to use in examining the crystalline structure of the minerals we hoped to get."

He sprinkled a pinch of the concrete on a glass slide, inserted it and sat down, his eye to the microscope. He turned the adjustment screws until he had the focus just right, then hunched over the eyepiece.

Presently Doug straightened up. "I can't be sure," he said, "but from the structure of the crystals, I'd say that the white powder is gypsum." His dark eyes went from Rick, to Tony, to Scotty, and his voice got harsh. "And that means that the failure of the dome—the defective concrete—was the result of carelessness."

"Maybe whoever mixed the cement was trying to make a bigger profit," Scotty suggested.

"Yes. And there's another possibility," Doug said.

Rick took a deep breath. Another possibility had occurred to him, too.

"There is a chance that this was deliberate sabotage!"

Rick leaned forward anxiously. That was the thought that had crossed his mind. All those "accidents" Doug had mentioned, the telegram, Cunner Stoles' agitating among the fishermen . . .

"Why do you say that?" Rick queried.

"I had some trouble with Jenkins, the contractor who built the domes. I found him trying to get into the process vault one day, and I'm afraid I got rather upset. We had words, and I'm sorry to say that I took a swing at him. I apologized later, of course, but he didn't seem appeased. He probably would have quit, but Tom talked him out of it. The thought came to me just now that perhaps he deliberately adulterated the cement in order to get even with me."

"Who was this Jenkins?" Rick asked.

The name seemed familiar, but of course it was a very common one. Only where had he heard it recently?

"A small contractor from New Haven," Doug replied.

"He approached us, and his price was so reasonable that we hired him. The job wasn't very complicated, since I made the forms for the domes myself—or, rather—supervised the carpenters who did. All Jenkins had to do was mix the cement and pour."

He rose and started out the door. Rick and Scotty fell in step. Tony followed behind. The foreman hadn't said a word. Rick wondered if Tony just didn't care, or whether he was simply a man of few words.

Examination of the dome showed that they had been very lucky, as Tony had said. The entire dome had not vanished, as Rick seemed to remember. There was only a hole, perhaps three feet square, where concrete had blown away from the reinforcing steel mesh up near the curve of the top. It had seemed such a terrific explosion because they had happened to be directly in front of the weak spot that gave under the pressure.

Water had poured from the hole; the initial spray had wetted the boys thoroughly, but they had hardly noticed. Most of the concrete blown out had crumbled into small pieces. Only one or two sizable chunks had been blown far. One of them had struck Doug.

Doug went to the second pressure dome and rubbed the surface. Rick had only to look at the engineer's face to know that it, too, had been sabotaged.

Silently Doug left them and walked down to the pier where the motorboat was tied. They saw him sit down and stare out to sea.

Tony departed in the direction of the pump house, and the boys were left alone.

"We might as well go back to the hut and sit down," Rick said. "Doug needs to be alone for a while, I guess."

Scotty looked at Tony Larzo's retreating form. "I don't think I could ever get real fond of Tony," he mused.

"That makes two of us," Rick agreed. "We can form a club. Do you suppose the domes were really sabotaged?"

"It beats me." Scotty shrugged. "There's something going on that we can't figure. Don't forget that telegram. And don't forget Cunner Stoles."

"They don't have to be connected," Rick pointed out as he stretched out on a bunk. "But while you're remembering not to forget things, include Mr. Fred Lewis."

"He and Cunner would make a good team." Scotty grinned. "Blubberpuss and paperpuss."

"Don't be disrespectful," Rick chided. "Say, I wonder what Tom will think about this?"

A voice spoke up from the doorway. "He'll probably philosophize about it. He's a great philosopher, Tom is."

The boys turned and saw Tom grinning at them.

"Now that you know how I'll react," he said, "suppose you tell me what it is?"

Rick searched for a gentle way to break the news.

"We had a little trouble," he said. "We were testing one of the pressure domes and it blew up."

All the humor went out of Tom's pleasant face. He sat down heavily and stared at them.

"Let's have it," he said. "All of it."

Rick told him the story briefly, ending with Doug's discovery of an adulterant in the concrete.

Tom was quiet for a long while, then he shook his head. "Where's Doug?"

"Sitting on the end of the pier."

"Did he try to get in touch with Jenkins?"

"No."

Tom went to the desk in the office part of the Quonset hut, searched through a file and came up with a slip of paper. "I think I'll see what he has to say," Tom said. He picked up the phone and gave the operator a New Haven number.

Rick and Scotty waited silently. Jenkins . . . Rick turned the name over in his mind again. Where had he heard it recently?

"Thanks," Tom said heavily, and hung up. He turned to the boys. "That number has been disconnected," he mimicked the telephone operator. "Isn't that just fine? Now what?" He sat down again. "How is Doug taking it?" he asked.

"Hard," Rick said. "I guess it's pretty serious."

"Plenty serious," Tom agreed. "I know you kids are interested, and I like the enthusiasm with which you pitched in, so I don't mind telling you. This thing, plus importing workmen from Bridgeport, is draining our remaining capital right down to the dregs." He paused, his face grave. "Just one more thing, and it doesn't have to be very big, will push us right over the edge into bankruptcy."

Rick and Scotty looked at him unbelievingly. They had had no intimation that the situation was that bad.

"It's true," Tom said quietly. "Unless we have a lot of luck from now on, this plant will never have a chance to start operations."

CHAPTER VI

Barby Bakes a Cake

"I NEED a suggestion," Tom Blakely said. "Something that will keep Doug's mind occupied, at least for to-night." He saw Rick's questioning glance and went on, "Doug's a pretty serious guy, and he's all wrapped up in this thing. Unless we figure out something that will keep him busy, he'll brood over it and get himself into a fine state of nerves."

That made sense to Rick. It fitted in with his feeling about Doug. The young engineer was as absorbed in the sea processing plant as Hartson Brant had always been in the Spindrift experiments.

Comparing Doug with his father gave Rick an idea. "I've got it," he exclaimed. "Do you suppose we could persuade Doug to fly down to Spindrift tonight? You could have dinner with us and stay the night."

"Just the thing," Tom said at once. "He'd like that, and I could talk him into it. Only how would we get there?"

"Steve Hollis's Fairchild," Rick answered promptly. "I can fly over and pick it up, then come back and get you. If Steve isn't planning to use it, of course."

"Call him and see," Tom said. "I'll get Doug. It will take a while to persuade him. He hates to get out of sight of the place."

It took only a minute to get a call through to the airport. Steve replied cheerfully that Rick was welcome to the Fairchild. "Of course you'll have to leave a tenthousand dollar deposit," he added.

"What luck," Rick replied. "I just happen to have that much in my piggy bank. You don't mind pennies, do you?"

"Certainly not. With that many pennies I can repave the runway with solid copper. Well, come and get it when you want it."

Rick hung up and grinned at Scotty. "A great guy if I ever met one."

In a few moments they heard the partners arguing outside. As they came into the hut, Tom said:

"Okay. Let's get down to cases. Just what's so important that you can't leave?"

"Well, I could do some wiring on the fractionator controls."

"You can be doing that while the workmen install the processing units. It wouldn't do any good to get the wiring done before then."

Doug was plainly weakening. "I could rig the chemical dumps."

"The platforms aren't built yet. So what good would it do?"

"None," Doug agreed with a grin.

"Then it's settled. Rick, we'll accept your invitation."

"Swell!" Rick exclaimed. "Scotty, better call up Cap'n Galt. We wouldn't want him to think we'd skipped without paying our bill. I'll call home from the airport to tell Mother we're coming."

"Okay," Scotty returned. "But you'd better change that shirt. Your mother would have a fit if she saw you like that."

Tom offered the loan of one of his, and Rick accepted. He changed, then hurried to the Cub, disconnected the warning system, warmed up, and headed for the airport. The obliging airport manager had the Fairchild waiting, the prop turning over. Rick exchanged his little plane for the big cabin biplane and was back at the beach landing strip in no time.

Scotty, Doug, and Tom were waiting on the beach. The partners had brought along an overnight bag, and now that the decision to go had been made, were excited at the prospect of visiting the famous island.

As the Fairchild took the air, Rick put it into a climbing turn directly over the plant. He glanced down and saw the hole in the pressure dome, and the thing that had been gnawing at his memory clicked into place.

"Listen! I know where I've heard the name of Jenkins before. It was on the return address of that envelope Fred Lewis dropped!"

"Who is Fred Lewis?" Tom asked.

"He's the man we saw at the plant gate on Sunday," Scotty explained. "We saw him again in the hotel lobby. Rick and I have some homework to do on that guy. But let's not get excited over the name on the envelope, Rick. Jenkins is pretty common. I know some people by that name myself."

Scotty was right, of course. The fact that he had seen the name of Jenkins on the envelope meant nothing. Rick put the matter out of his mind and concentrated on his flying. Instead of flying down the coastline as he usually did, he set a compass course for Brooklyn, then crossed over Staten Island and picked up the New Jersey coast. In an incredibly short time, to one used to the lazy flight of the Cub, Spindrift Island came in sight.

"So that's Spindrift!" Doug's voice sounded awed.

Rick winked at Scotty. He knew from the excitement in the young engineer's voice that the troubles at the plant had been forgotten, at least for a while.

They landed on the grassy strip along the edge of the orchard and Rick set the parking brakes and cut the engine.

"Welcome to Spindrift," he said proudly.

The engine noise gave way to furious barks. A shaggy little form came pelting through the orchard, teeth bared and ready to defend the island against all invaders.

Rick stepped out and jumped down from the wing.

"And who are you barking at?" he demanded sternly.

Dismal's throat clogged in mid-bark. He yipped joyously, then rolled over and played dead.

Scotty sniffed the air. "Not bad, that mixture of skunk and lavender. I guess Barby sprayed him with foo-foo, all right."

Barby herself came running toward them, a slim figure in tennis skirt and one of Rick's shirts.

"Rick! Where did you get the new plane? Hi, Scotty. Golly, it's beautiful!"

Then she saw the two strangers just getting out of the plane and was suddenly very dignified.

"Barby," Rick said, "Mr. Douglas Chambers and Mr. Thomas Blakely. Doug and Tom, this is my sister Barbara."

"How do you do," Barby said graciously, her eyes bright with curiosity.

"How do you do, Miss Brant." Tom smiled, but Doug's greeting was just a polite murmur. His attention had been instantly focused on the gray bulk of the laboratories.

Mr. and Mrs. Brant came to meet them as they walked to the porch, their cordial welcome making the partners feel instantly at home. Mrs. Brant promised one of her excellent dinners, and, followed reluctantly by Barby, she went off to the kitchen. The boys joined

Hartson Brant and the partners in a tour of the island and the labs.

Not until they were settled on the porch after dinner did conversation turn to the sea mine plant, and then it was the partners who brought up the subject.

"You must be curious about what we're doing, Mr. Brant," Tom ventured.

"Naturally." Hartson Brant smiled. "I know something of the standard methods of processing sea water, but I understand you have something entirely new."

Doug nodded. "I started to explain to Rick, but . . ."

"But it was too much for me." Rick grinned. "All about molecular electronic coefficients, and stuff."

He was startled at the swift change in his father's expression. The scientist leaned forward, eyes wide. "Do you mean to tell me you've solved the necessary equations for that?"

"Yes, sir," Doug said with a note of pride in his voice. "I got on the track while I was in school, but it wasn't until I read the reports on atomic chain reaction and the cadmium factor that I had any luck. I had already figured out how we could process sea water by using the electronic characteristics of the various molecules of the compounds in solution. Then, when the atom reports put me on the track, I was able to figure out the electronic coefficients. I'd like you to see my equation tables someday, sir."

"I'd like to," Hartson Brant said. "How are you using them?"

"Well, the electronic equipment, except for individual control panels, is centered in one building. We prepare the water in fractionators by using a fractional distillation process in the presence of catalysts, then we electrolyze it as much as possible in pressure domes, and finally treat it chemically in the sediment tanks. Then it goes to the electronic processors and the equations work in at that point. After that it's routine."

"Very sound," Hartson Brant declared. "And evolved from a brilliant theory. On the basis of what you've just told me, Douglas, I think we might extend an invitation to you to join us here at Spindrift at any time you feel free to do so."

Rick sat back, speechless. He had heard polite refusals given men who wanted to join the Spindrift scientists. He had never heard, or expected to hear, anyone actually invited to join! He looked at Doug with new respect.

"Holy leaping porpoises," Scotty exclaimed, "if those processes are that good, we shouldn't leave them alone like that!"

"Never fear," Tom said, "they're well guarded. That little concrete house is built like a bank vault, but better. Inside the concrete is armor plate four inches thick that we got from Navy surplus. It would take an atom bomb to break in."

"That's a relief," Rick murmured. His thoughts had paralleled Scotty's.

"Now, I have some questions," Hartson Brant said. "I'm interested in the business side."

"That's my department," Tom Blakely said. "You've probably guessed that we're operating on a shoestring. Any of the big companies would have backed us, but we didn't want to share the processes. Amalgamated Mines has approached us several times. Doug went to them originally and they wanted to buy the processes outright, at a ridiculous price. Well, I had a little money I'd inherited, and Doug had some. We pooled that, and Doug's uncle invested another ten thousand."

"Uncle Frank has a big fortune," Doug interposed, "but he doesn't believe in gambling, or so he says. He refused to put in any more than ten thousand."

"Anyway," Tom continued, "we got going and established credit. We had enough capital to start small. But things began to happen. Costs went up, and so did wages."

He went on to outline the mishaps that had befallen the partners, and concluded: "Now the situation is really serious. Our credit is running out and our capital has dwindled. After we pay the workmen and rebuild the domes, we'll be almost broke. One more accident would finish us."

After a moment's silence, Hartson Brant asked: "Are you familiar with probability mathematics?"

"A little," Doug said.

"They're a hobby of mine," the scientist explained. "Probabilities work in a measurable sequence. For instance, I could predict with some accuracy just which cards will turn up in a game of solitaire, after I've seen the first few. Now, in constructing anything like your plant, certain numbers of accidents are probable. But from what you tell me, and knowing something of similar plants, I'd say that you have exceeded your mathematical quota."

Rick felt Scotty tense beside him. Doug and Tom were staring at the scientist.

"In other words," Hartson Brant went on, "I accept what you've told me as almost certain mathematical proof that many of your troubles have been man-made!"

Doug and Tom glanced at each other.

"We've thought of that," Tom said.

"So have I," Rick echoed.

"Ditto," Scotty said.

"But who would have cause to sabotage us?" Doug asked.

Hartson Brant countered with another question. "Who would get the processes if you went bankrupt?"

"Our creditors," Tom answered promptly. "But they're all respected firms."

"Well, it's one answer," Hartson Brant said. He rose from his chair. "I think we've talked enough for a bit. Is anyone game for a walk?"

Only Doug seemed to have that much ambition. He and the scientist departed in the direction of the tidal flats.

Barby and Mrs. Brant appeared, their after-dinner chores finished.

"I'm sorry we haven't any cake for your usual late snack," Mrs. Brant said to Scotty, her eyes twinkling. "But we didn't expect you."

"Barby will bake us a cake," Scotty offered.

Barby glared at him.

Rick grinned. Barby could bake cakes, all right, but she hated cooking. It wasn't sophisticated, she said.

"Sure," he agreed. "She makes wonderful cakes, Tom. Let's all go into the kitchen and help her."

Barby knew when she was trapped, but she made a last try at resisting.

"But that would be so dull, Rick!"

"Not at all." Tom smiled. "It's so unusual to find a girl who can really cook these days!"

Barby's resistance to the idea melted. "All right, then," she said gaily, "let's bake a cake!"

Mrs. Brant said something under her breath that sounded to Rick like: "I never thought I'd see the day." But she raised no objection.

They all gathered in the kitchen and offered advice while Barby mixed the ingredients.

Then Rick got a sudden brain storm and nudged Scotty.

"Tell you what, sis, you make the cake and I'll bake it in my induction heater."

It was a unit that he had rigged for cooking hamburgers late at night when he wanted a snack. It worked like an induction furnace, high-frequency current cooking anything placed between the two coils.

Barby fell neatly into the trap. "Oh, would you, Rick? Then we won't have to bother with the oven."

He had cooked things for her before and she knew that the induction coils took less time.

"I'll help him," Scotty said, on his toes because of the nudge Rick had given him. He knew something was afoot and was ready to help out. "Tell you what, you and Tom fix the frosting while we bake the cake."

Barby mixed the batter and folded it neatly into an oblong tin. Rick, unnoticed, had gotten an identical tin from the cupboard. He walked out with it hidden under his jacket, and in a moment Scotty followed with Barby's cake.

Once in the safety of Rick's room, Scotty asked: "What's on your mind? Dirty work of some kind, I'll bet."

Rick produced the second tin. "Barby always makes a loaf cake. That was what gave me the idea."

He connected the induction coils and put the cake in between them. It would be done in five minutes. Then he rummaged around in a box of odds and ends and came up with a balloon.

"Watch this," he said gleefully. He blew up the balloon, which was one of the long sausage-shaped variety, stopping when it was about the size of the cake tin. He tied a knot to hold in the air, then placed the inflated balloon in the cake tin, squeezing until it just fitted, the red rubber protruding in a mound, like the top of a cake.

"Now," he directed, "run downstairs and get the frosting. Tell Barby we'll reverse the current and cool the cake so we can frost it right away."

"But that's impossible," Scotty objected.

Rick grinned. "Barby doesn't know that. Tell her to entertain Tom and leave everything to us. And get a cake plate."

"Got it," Scotty answered, and hurried off while Rick kept an eye on the cake in the induction cooker.

The cake was done when Scotty returned, carrying a bowl of thick white frosting and a cake plate. "I convinced her," he reported. "She thinks you're a second Edison, being able to cool a cake in an induction heater."

Rick took the cake out of the heater and transferred it from the cake tin to the plate. Then he turned on a fan and left it to cool. "There's plenty of frosting," he said. "We'll frost the cake later."

"It smells good," Scotty said yearningly.

Rick took the bowl of frosting and carefully coated the balloon until the last trace of red rubber had vanished under a tempting coat of white. The balloon in the tin made a slightly higher mound than a real cake, but otherwise there was no outward difference. The frosting was already hardening.

"Let's go," Rick said. "We'll leave the real one up here and come back for it later. Did they go out to the porch?"

"Yes," Scotty said, grinning.

They hurried down the stairs and carried the frosted balloon out to the porch.

"A beauty," Rick remarked, holding it out. "A real masterpiece. And light as a feather. Lighter, maybe."

Scotty stifled a betraying chuckle.

Barby's eyes opened wide. "Did you cool it that fast? Rick! You didn't take it out of the tin!"

Rick looked properly surprised. "Gosh, am I a dope! Well, never mind. We'll serve it from the tin. Do we get milk with it?"

Barby looked at the cake doubtfully, but didn't say anything further. She hurried to the kitchen.

Mrs. Brant looked at her son suspiciously. "You have something up your sleeves, both of you. You look much too smug."

"I didn't know you could reverse an induction heater," Tom said thoughtfully.

"Oh, sure," Rick said hurriedly. "I'll tell you about it later."

Barby reappeared with a tray containing a pitcher of milk, glasses, and plates for the cake.

"I think Tom should cut the cake," Scotty said. "He rates the honor as the only visitor present."

"Of course," Rick said. He picked up the cake tin and set it before Tom on a coffee table. He had to be careful not to let anyone else handle it because of its giveaway lightness. He presented the cake knife to Tom.

"Cut," he invited.

Barby watched anxiously.

Tom took the knife, and with a smile at Barby, started to cut. Rick almost laughed outright at the strange look that came over his face, but he choked it back.

"Harder," he urged. "It must be sponge cake."

The knife penetrated the hard outer coating of white frosting but wouldn't cut.

"Sponge cake," Scotty agreed, and started coughing. Rick poked him and he regained his self-control.

Tom gave the boys a worried look. The cake just wouldn't cut.

"Jab it," Rick suggested. He stole a look at Barby's horrified, scarlet face.

Tom had been gently trying to cut into the cake, but now he took the blunt cake knife and poked. Nothing happened, except that the knife pushed right back at him. Tom looked like a man who had just had a sand-wich bite him back.

Rick felt as though he would burst from the effort of controlling his mirth, but he felt in his pocket and came out with the scout knife he always carried. He opened the long blade and handed it to Tom.

"Try this," Rick suggested.

Mrs. Brant was holding a handkerchief to her lips, but a soft giggle escaped. She looked accusingly at Rick.

Barby and Scotty were both crimson, but for different reasons.

Tom took the knife with an embarrassed smile, and poked. Air whooshed out at him and he almost jumped out of his seat.

Rick waited for the cake to collapse, as a punctured balloon should. But it didn't!

"What on earth . . ." Mrs. Brant started.

Scotty fell into a chair and roared.

Rick stared at the cake tin. He had seen instantly what had happened. The balloon had collapsed as the air rushed out through the hole Tom had made, but the hardened frosting had remained intact. He looked at it and a picture flashed into his mind, a picture from a newsreel. Men were pouring cement over a domelike rubber bag . . .

"The pressure domes," he said, his voice hushed. "They could be rebuilt like that!"

"What?" Tom asked in bewilderment.

"Rick, what did you do to my cake?" Barby demanded, almost tearfully.

"They build houses," Rick said. "I saw it in the newsreel! They pour concrete over a rubber mold, let it harden, and then deflate the mold!"

Tom was on his feet now. "Yes! Gosh, yes! I've seen pictures of it in the magazines! If we could get one of those firms to re-pour the domes just as they would a house . . ."

Suddenly Tom was off the porch, running in the direction Doug and Hartson Brant had gone, and he was yelling Doug's name at the top of his voice.

"That's what I like about this place," Barby said unhappily. "Even the guests are crazy." She was staring at the cake.

Rick and Scotty shook hands soberly.

"That's using the old bean," Scotty said. "They can save plenty of money, and have the domes re-poured in a single day!"

Mrs. Brant stood beside them. "You'll get around to explaining, I'm sure. But, meanwhile, what about Barby's cake?"

Rick was instantly contrite. "We'll have it right now." As Scotty went to get the real cake, he explained: "It was supposed to be a joke, sis. But it turned out to be the luckiest thing ever." He explained about the pressure domes and how houses were made by using the rubber forms.

Barby was mollified by the explanation. Then suddenly she laughed. "It would have been a howl if the cake had collapsed." She poked the crust of frosting with her finger and it cracked and fell into the tin.

Then they were all laughing.

CHAPTER VII

Cunner Has a Visitor

WEDNESDAY passed rapidly after the four returned from
Spindrift Island. Tom departed at once, with several
errands to perform. First, he had to contract for the
rebuilding of the domes by a house construction firm, if
he could. Then he intended calling on a lawyer friend
in New Haven, to discuss instituting a search for
Jenkins, with an eye to a possible damage suit. His third
job was to see if the employment agency he had visited
the day before had succeeded in making arrangements
for workmen.

Rick, as soon as he returned the Fairchild and staked
down the Cub on the beach, went to work on the fractionator control panel, a highly complex arrangement
of switches and relays that operated an even more complex rack of electronic controls. Familiar as Rick was
with such items, some of the circuits were beyond him.

But he did as he was told and tried not to bother Doug with too many questions, and the work proceeded rapidly.

Tony and Scotty spent the day cleaning chrome-alloy sediment tanks, a job that meant plenty of work with rag and brush and solvent.

Tom returned as they were cleaning up. He was jubilant with news of a successful day. The employment agency had promised them forty men, to start on Monday morning. His lawyer friend had taken over the Jenkins case. And a firm that poured concrete houses had promised him an answer before tomorrow noon.

He had one more bit of news.

"We're taking no more chances, Doug. I've hired some special guards from a private agency at New Haven. They'll patrol the place from five in the evening until we open in the morning, taking turns. And they'll be armed. It'll cost money, but I think it's better to take no risks."

"You're right, Tom," Doug assented. "When do they start?"

"Friday night."

"We'll take turns standing guard tonight," Rick offered.

Doug gave them a warm smile. "Thanks a lot, kids. But with Tom and me sleeping here, I don't think we'll have any trouble. The time when we'll really need the guards is when we tear the fence down."

That was news to Rick and Scotty. They looked at the partners blankly.

"Economy," Tom explained. "We talked it over last night. We'll need lumber for the tank shacks and chemical platforms and we just can't afford to buy any. So we'll have to use the fence."

Rick and Scotty discussed it as they hiked into town.

"I guess when Tom said bankrupt, he wasn't kidding," Scotty mused.

"It must be hard on them," Rick said.

"Tough," Scotty agreed.

"I wish we could help more."

Scotty shrugged. "So do I. But what can we do? Except keep our eyes open."

An idea was turning over in the back of Rick's head, but he didn't say anything. They walked up the steps and into the hotel lobby, and Rick hesitated at the sight of Fred Lewis reading a newspaper in one of the uncomfortable chairs. Was it imagination or did the man lift the paper higher, as though afraid they might get a good look at him?

The boys cleaned up, then went downstairs to the restaurant for supper. Over omelettes and French fried potatoes, Rick told Scotty what had been on his mind.

"I'm wondering about Cunner Stoles. Do you suppose he's spreading rumors just out of meanness, as Cap'n Galt says, or is he doing it for a purpose?"

"Search me," Scotty said.

"I wish we could find out."

"Maybe we can."

"You read my mind." Rick grinned. "Were you thinking maybe we could keep an eye on him?"

"Why not? We haven't any other plans for the evening."

"It's a date," Rick said. He wasn't sure it would do any good, but if there were a sure-enough plot against the sea mine, it was time they did something about it.

After supper they went back to their room to wait until it was dark out of doors. While Scotty read a magazine, sprawled out on his bed in solid comfort, Rick wrote a letter to Chahda, bringing the Hindu boy up to date on recent happenings.

"Listen, did you bring sneakers with you?" Rick asked when he had finished. It was dark now.

"Sure."

"You'd better wear them."

Scotty put the magazine down. "You're not a scientist, chum, you're a frustrated Dick Tracy. You get more kick out of trailing some innocent character than you do out of a nice clean experiment like the moon rocket."

"You don't, of course."

"I do it for the exercise," Scotty said. He swung off the bed and went to the closet. He found sneakers and put them on. Rick followed suit.

"It's dark enough," Rick said.

"I guess so. Let's go down the back way. No point in advertising things to the whole hotel."

It was a sensible suggestion. The back stairs led down into a dark courtyard where restaurant supplies and similar items were delivered. The boys had discovered them the first night when Scotty made a wrong turn and almost fell down them.

In a moment they were out of doors and making their way toward the water front through the back alleys. If they found Cunner, it probably would be down at Zukky's restaurant.

"What do we do when we locate him?" Rick asked.

"Just stick with him until he hits the hay, I guess," Scotty said. "It wouldn't do much good to sandbag him."

They fell silent again, and in a few moments came out on the boardwalk at the water front. It was almost entirely dark in this part of town. The fishermen had secured for the night: their draggers were tied up along the fingerlike piers. Only the spotty light from Zukky's broke the darkness.

Rick made his way along the boardwalk until he reached a spot where he could look in through the dingy windows. His heart gave a leap when he saw Cunner seated at the counter, a glass in front of him.

"There's our boy," he whispered.

"I see him. Not many people in there."

"Stay back and duck into the shadows if you hear anyone coming."

"Don't worry, I will."

The minutes ticked by with agonizing slowness. Rick watched Cunner until his eyes ached. Now and then the pudgy fisherman glanced at his wrist watch.

"He's waiting for someone," Rick guessed.

"Looks like it," Scotty agreed.

They were silent again. Rick shifted his weight from one foot to the other and began to feel foolish. After all, what could they hope to accomplish?

Suddenly Scotty gripped Rick's arm. Cunner Stoles had glanced at his wrist watch and pushed his glass away. With a word to the counterman, he started toward the door. The boys melted into the shadows and moved around a corner of the building.

Cunner came out to the boardwalk, stood for a moment in front of the restaurant, and consulted his watch again. Then he turned and walked right past where the boys were hiding. Rick automatically ducked his head so that the fisherman couldn't see the white blur of his face.

Their quarry walked a few yards down the boardwalk, then turned onto one of the long piers. Rick and Scotty waited until the echo of his footsteps had died away, then they slipped silently after him.

They passed boats that made a darker bulk against the blackness of the water, and they heard the tide lapping at the piles under their feet.

Up ahead, a dim light, like a kerosene lamp, flickered, then settled down to a steady glow. The boys crept cautiously toward it and saw that it came from the cabin of a ramshackle dragger. Evidently this was Cunner's boat.

Hugging the far side of the pier, they neared it, came opposite, and saw Cunner seated in the cabin, lighting his pipe. Rick took Scotty's arm and led him on past, out to the very end of the pier.

He put his lips to Scotty's ear and whispered, "Does he live there or is he waiting for someone?"

"Must be waiting. Otherwise he wouldn't've looked at his watch."

"That's how I figure it. Let's get comfortable."

There was a pile of lobster pots at the end of the pier. They sat down and began the wait. The water was close under them and the air had the scent peculiar to water fronts, a not unpleasing mixture of salt mud flats, tarred rope, engine fuel, and a faint but definite fishiness.

Rick's eyes were accustomed to the darkness now, and he could make out Scotty's features. If he could see, he reasoned, so could anyone else.

"If he gets a visitor, duck behind the lobster pots," he whispered.

"Check," Scotty nodded.

Somewhere out in the bay a fish broke water, but aside from the constant murmur of the water that was the only sound. Inland, the town made a glow in the sky, and to their left Rick could see lights that might have been from the plant.

Scotty tensed, then Rick heard it, too, the measured tread of someone coming down the boardwalk. The footsteps hesitated at their pier, then came toward them. Instantly they were behind the pile of lobster pots, scarcely breathing.

The footsteps reached the spot where Cunner's boat was tied. Rick peered out from behind his shield and dimly made out a dark figure. Then it moved into the light from Cunner's window and he sucked in his breath sharply.

Cunner's visitor was Fred Lewis!

Rick's fingers sank into Scotty's arm.

"I see him," Scotty breathed.

Lewis went aboard and the cabin door slammed. On the echo, Rick was moving, Scotty right with him. Crouching low they moved down the pier, treading carefully for fear of loose boards.

There was a murmur of voices from inside and in a moment they could make out words.

". . . don't want to risk being seen with you . . . only stay a minute . . ."

Rick edged closer. Lewis had a voice that was oddly familiar. It was the voice of one used to giving orders. "You have to do better, Stoles. It isn't enough for the men to refuse to work. They must be stirred up to the point of violence."

Cunner's voice was a low growl with a whining note in it.

"It ain't as easy as that. They know the law about

dumpin' poison. It ain't no cinch to convince 'em."

"Keep working on it. We'll see that they're convinced. Now get this straight, Stoles . . ."

This was the evidence they had needed! Lewis had lowered his voice, and Rick crept nearer. He had to hear every bit of that conversation. He was perilously close to the cabin, but he was careful not to make a sound, not even to breathe hard. He felt Scotty close to him.

Lewis's voice was so low-pitched he couldn't make out the words. He moved closer, bent forward, straining to hear, and his toe caught on the edge of the pier!

Rick went over headfirst and landed sprawling on the deck of the boat. His arm, outflung to break his fall, struck an empty gasoline can that crashed against the cabin with an appalling racket that brought the hair on his head up straight. He struggled to his feet and promptly fell flat again, his legs tangled in a coil of loose rope. Scotty's hand pulled at his collar and he tried to get upright. For an awful moment he felt as though pythons had him in a death grip.

Not more than two seconds had passed, but there was bedlam inside the cabin, and the door flew open. Light streamed out onto the deck. Rick fought the coils of rope and saw Scotty rush by him, saw Cunner step on deck, saw Scotty hurtle into him like a blocking fullback. Cunner went back into the cabin with a crash, carrying Lewis with him.

Scotty's strong arm pulled Rick to his feet. He shook off the coil of rope.

Footsteps were pounding down the boardwalk. The noise was bringing someone from the restaurant!

There was only one way of escape. Already Cunner was coming out of the cabin again, but with more caution this time.

"Get going," Scotty whispered urgently.

Rick sucked in his breath and dove. The water enveloped him. He stayed under, swimming toward the next pier. When he came up, he heard yells from the pier they had just left. Scotty's head bobbed to the surface next to him.

"Straight ahead," Scotty gasped. "Miss the piers and stay under as much as you can. They're manning a searchlight."

The swim was a nightmare. Rick stayed under until his lungs burned, then he came to the top, rolling like a seal to see if light were playing on the surface. Once he had to wait until the beam passed, and thought his lungs would burst.

Then they passed the last pier and angled toward shore.

Scotty swam close. "How you making it?"

"All right," Rick said briefly.

"Try to keep going until we get near the plant. It's not far."

It wasn't far when you said it quickly, but it seemed

eternity before they got to the underwater bulk of the sea inlet. Rick gave thanks a dozen times that they had worn sneakers. Leather shoes would have been too heavy, and they would have had to drop them.

Then, at last, they were walking up past the inlet pipe, breathing deeply, too relieved to do more than grin at each other.

There were lights in the Quonset hut. They ran to the door and knocked.

Tom opened the door, then his eyes opened even wider. "Come in," he said. "Come in."

Doug rose as they entered. "Good gosh, what happened?"

"A little swim," Scotty managed.

"That's nice," Tom said. "Did you take a bar of soap with you?"

"No time," Rick said. He sank down in a chair and let the water drip from him. It was easy enough to joke now that it was over.

"Get out of those clothes," Doug directed. He found an electric heater and plugged it in. "Good thing we saved this. We used it on cool nights last month."

In a short time the boys were wrapped in blankets, their clothes drying on chair backs, and they were busily drinking hot cocoa. Only when the cocoa was down did Doug permit them to talk.

"Now," he said, "let's have it."

The story didn't take long to tell. Rick quoted the bit

of conversation they had heard, with verification from Scotty.

Doug and Tom gave each other a long look.

"You'll take no more chances," Tom said decisively. Then his warm grin flashed. "But I'm glad you did this time, as long as you got out of it all right. Now we know for sure what we're up against, even if we don't know who the enemy is."

"Stoles and Lewis," Scotty said.

"I don't know Lewis, of course, but I'll bet he is only a part of it," Tom remarked.

"That's my thought," Doug said. "Now, what do we do about it?"

"We can't have them arrested, I suppose." Rick ventured.

"Not a chance." Scotty was definite. "What we heard wouldn't convince a jury of old ladies, even if it did convince us."

"Anyway," Rick said stoutly, "we're making progress."

"Yes," Scotty cracked. "From well-dressed detective to blanket Indian in ten minutes flat."

CHAPTER VIII

The Playing Gets Rough

THE partners were just finishing breakfast when Rick and Scotty arrived at the plant the following morning.

"Well, if it isn't the moonlight bathers," Tom greeted them.

"There wasn't any moonlight," Doug said.

"See the scientific mind in action?" Tom grinned. "Always a stickler for the precise fact. I was only speaking poetically."

"Never mind." Doug smiled. "Let's put that energy to work instead of wasting it on oratory."

Tony Larzo stuck his head in the door. "What first?"

"Bolt up that panel by fractionator one," Doug directed. "Rick and I will start work on that this morning."

Scotty watched Tony pick up a box of tools and depart, then he asked, "How much stuff needs to be done before the plant gets into operation?"

Rick had been curious about that, too.

"The domes, of course," Doug began. "You know about those. If the company phones in an okay this morning, we can expect to have them up and rewired by the end of next week. Then there are the fractionators. Rick and I can finish wiring them today and tomorrow."

"Carstairs should have the units ready," Tom said thoughtfully. "I think I'll take a trip into Bridgeport today and see about them."

"The fractionator boxes are empty now," Doug explained. "But it won't take long to install and connect the units, once they're delivered. Then we have to rig the chemical platforms and dumps. They're the platforms that will hold the tanks of chemicals over the sediment tanks. When we want to add anything to the sea water, we'll just turn a valve."

"And mix until done," Tom said. "The mixing arrangement was my idea. I'm a scientist, too."

"What did you do," Rick asked with a grin, "invent a better egg beater?"

Doug smiled. "Just about. I wanted to use wooden paddles, agitated by hand, but Tom showed up one day with an electric outboard motor. It runs on twelve volts. Fishermen use them for trolling, I understand. But they'll work fine for us. We'll just hang one on the edge of each tank and pretend we're fishing."

"Smart," Scotty complimented. "I've seen them advertised in sporting magazines. Well, is that all that has to be done?"

"Not quite. We need an exhaust pipe for waste water. The workmen can install that in a day." Doug rose and picked up the kit that contained his tools. "Rick, you'll work with me. Scotty, you can continue cleaning the tanks. Tony will bear a hand as soon as he finishes at the fractionators."

Scotty departed in the direction of the tanks and Tom hunted for a necktie to wear into town. Rick fell in step with Doug and they walked down to the square concrete boxes where the fractional process would take place.

"Isn't there anything to do in there?" Rick asked, indicating the vaultlike building that housed the central processes.

"Nothing but minor adjustments. That was the first thing I did. It took two months of hard work."

"I think I'm beginning to see how it works," Rick said. "Those electronic coefficients duplicate the electrical structure of the molecules in the minerals you want to get."

"That's right," Doug said. "But it isn't an exact duplication. We leave enough difference in structure to form a potential. Do you understand that?"

Rick thought it over. "I think so. Like in a storage battery. That's what makes the current flow—a difference in potential between the positive and negative plates."

"That's a good way of expressing it. Well, the potential we set up between our electronic circuit and the mineral we're after is just enough to separate the mineral from the water. So the mineral gathers around the electrodes of the circuit."

"And you just scrape off the gold or silver," Rick finished.

Doug laughed. "You make it sound so easy. Actually, there's a lot more to it than that, but you're getting on to the basic idea."

As they reached the square fractionator boxes, Tony looked up from putting his tools in the box. "All done. What now?"

"Help Scotty at the sediment tanks."

"Okay," Tony grunted.

"There goes a man of very few words," Rick said as Tony left them.

"He's a good worker, though," Doug told him. "Well, let's see what we have."

Tony had bolted steel uprights together at the side of the concrete box numbered "1." The uprights supported what looked like the painted aluminum chassis for a radio set. They were to install the electronic control equipment on which they had worked yesterday in there, wire in the instruments, and connect them to the circuits that led into the fractionator itself.

While Doug consulted his wiring diagrams, Rick took a look at the concrete structure. A six-inch pipe led into one side. Evidently that was for the sea water.

At the bottom were other, smaller pipes that would lead the water out after treatment. The valves for all the pipes were outside, since the concrete structure would be full of water when in operation.

There were no windows, of course, and only one door —if it could be called a door. It was like the door on a big safe, swinging on its massive hinges until it fitted flush into the opening. A thick rubber gasket made the door waterproof, and it could be sealed shut by turning a wheel on the outside.

Rick spun the wheel with the door open and saw steel fingers about an inch in diameter push out around the rim of the door. The fingers would fit into receptacles in the doorframe, sealing it against anything but a blast of explosive. The locking mechanism was protected on the inside from the water by a stainless steel plate set on a rubber gasket.

He stooped low and went into the box. Projecting, threaded rods showed him where the fractionator units were to be installed. There were evidently four of them. High on one wall was the inlet pipe. Lower down, the outlets thrust through, ready to be connected. The entire inside was coated with the same hard, shiny plastic Doug had used inside the pressure domes.

Doug called to him and he went out. They pored over the wiring diagrams while the soldering irons heated, and then they went to work.

The wiring was complex, but it went smoothly under

Doug's guidance. They took time out for a brief lunch and then went right back at it again. Scotty reported that they would finish cleaning the tanks by nightfall.

"A messy job," he said. "We have to dig off the transparent stuff they coated the sides with to protect the chrome finish. First we scrape, then we wipe with solvent. Not hard, but tiresome."

Late in the afternoon, Tom returned with both good and bad news. He came to where Doug and Rick were working and gave them the good news first.

"The construction company will have a crew out here next Tuesday to pour the domes, and the price is even lower than I expected."

The bad news was that, while the Carstairs Company had the fractionator units ready, they had hedged when he asked about delivery. They wanted to see both the partners tomorrow afternoon.

Doug looked grave.

"What does that mean?" Rick asked.

"That our credit has run out. We're going to have to do some fast talking." Tom addressed Doug. "I've made a date with Kent for tonight. We'll run over the books, so we'll know just how we stand before we see Carstairs."

"Kent is an accountant who has been working on the books with Tom," Doug explained. "But, Tom, we can't leave the plant unprotected. The guards don't start until tomorrow night."

Rick spoke up instantly. "Scotty and I will stand by for you."

Tom grinned. "That was what I had hoped. Thanks. It won't be more than a couple of hours. You can go into town and eat, then come back about seven. We'll leave then."

Doug put his hand on Rick's shoulder. "I don't know what we'd do without you two."

"But no detecting," Tom cautioned. "We don't want you eager beavers to get into a jam you might not be able to get out of."

"No detecting," Rick promised. "It's too wet. We found that out last night."

Scotty walked to the door of the Quonset hut. "It's almost dark out."

Rick looked up from the magazine *Electronics* he had borrowed from Doug. "They should be back before long. What time is it?"

"Half past eight. They won't be back much before ten, I bet. What are they doing, anyway?"

"Getting ready to give Carstairs a battle," Rick said, putting the magazine down. He joined Scotty at the door.

"This finance stuff is beyond me," Scotty said. "What's it all about? Why should Carstairs hold up delivery?"

"They're afraid they won't get paid," Rick explained.

THE PLAYING GETS ROUGH

"It's because new plants like this get started on credit. They buy the stuff, to be paid for when they get operating."

"You mean the manufacturers give you the stuff with which to make the money to pay them back?"

"That's it. Sounds queer, but it always works that way. But they only let you have the equipment if your credit is good. Now Tom and Doug are close to being broke, and I guess their credit isn't good any more. So Carstairs has doubts about getting paid."

Scotty had stopped listening and was staring down toward the water front.

"What is it?" Rick asked quickly.

"Thought I saw a light."

Rick stepped close to the screen, straining to see. After a moment he caught the faintest suggestion of a flickering light down beyond the sediment tanks.

"I saw it," Rick said softly. "Down by the fractionators."

The boys looked at each other. The gate was closed, and they hadn't heard it open. Silently Scotty reached under the table and picked up a heavy, steel pinch bar. Rick found an electric lantern of the type that holds two dry cell batteries.

"No noise," he whispered.

Scotty nodded and slipped out through the screen door, Rick right behind him. Rick's heart was beating fast. If they caught a prowler, they might be able to get the answers to some of their questions about the troubles at the plant. He motioned toward the process vault. Scotty moved silently into its shadow and Rick joined him, peering around the corner.

He saw the light again, a thin beam like that of a pencil flashlight. It was partially shielded by the fractionator panel. The thought leaped into his mind that someone was trying to destroy the work they had done that day. He left the shelter of the process vault and ran, picking up a sizable rock as he went. There was no idea of concealment now. They couldn't let that wiring job be destroyed!

Scotty ran at his side, the pinch bar held ready. Rick called to him: "Be careful!" They reached the fractionators and ran around them, their weapons raised.

There was no one in sight.

Rick stopped and switched on the electric lantern. The beam cut a white swath through the night down to the water front. He flashed it around, searching for a sign of the prowler.

"Don't see him," Scotty said.

Rick switched off the light and waited. After a second he heard the sound of brush crunching under running feet, a sound that came from outside the fence.

"He's gone!" Scotty exclaimed. "He must have heard us and beat it down to the water front and skipped around the fence. Do we go after him?"

Rick considered. "No," he said finally. "We shouldn't

leave the plant. Let's look around and see what he was after."

He turned on his light and shot it at the fractionator control panel, but it seemed intact. To make sure, he opened the back and looked in at the circuits. The wiring had not been disturbed.

"Funny," he mused. "What do you suppose he was after?"

He walked back to the front of the concrete structure and shot his light around. It came to rest on the door.

"Open," he said. "We closed it." He shot the light inside, and the rays gleamed on something metallic.

"What is it?" Then Scotty gasped. "Looks like a dynamite cap."

Rick was already going through the door, his light on the coppery thing.

"Careful," Scotty urged, pushing in behind him. "We may have got here just as he was fixing to blow up the fractionators."

Rick knelt and Scotty crouched beside him. It was a dynamite cap, all right, but it wasn't connected to anything. Scotty reached out and picked it up. "No fuse, no dynamite. What the heck do you suppose . . ."

They whirled suddenly as air pushed against them.

"Hey!" Scotty yelled, and threw himself forward.

Too late! The door slapped into place and there was a click as the bolts shot home.

They were trapped!

Both boys threw their weight against the door, once, twice, then Rick called a halt.

"No use. We couldn't open it with a battering ram."

Scotty straightened up. "What a pair of saps," he moaned. "There were two of them, and they mouse-trapped us! They can wreck the place while we're in here."

Rick, too, had seen at once what had happened. One man had run away, deliberately making enough noise to be heard. The second man had waited in the darkness, perhaps behind the second fractionator, until they found the dynamite cap and went in to investigate. Then it had been a simple thing to slam the door shut and bolt it. Even now the other man would be coming back, and they could wreck the unprotected plant at leisure.

"Cunner and Lewis," he said bitterly.

"Who else? Rick, there must be a way out."

Rick shot the light around without comment, showing Scotty that the door was the only way.

"Listen," Scotty said suddenly. "Did you hear anything?"

Rick tensed, holding his breath. After a moment he heard it faintly through the heavy walls. The noise of the pump engine! On its heels came a gurgle that made his heart almost stop.

Water!

As he shot the electric lantern at the inlet water started to gush out. Then they were ducking back against the nearest wall while salt water poured into the concrete box and splashed against their legs.

Rick turned his light downward, to the outlet pipes. The water would run right out again . . .

But the rising flood passed the outlets and kept rising. The outlets were closed!

"We've got to get out or we'll be drowned," he gasped.

"But how?" Scotty's voice was almost lost in the roar of the water.

The door was the only way. Rick crouched beside it, shooting his light over it. The rubber seal protruded a little, but that was no help. He remembered the steel bolts that had thrust out when he turned the wheel that morning.

"The locking mechanism," Scotty yelled. "Can we get at it?"

The steel plate Rick had noticed was secured by a dozen screw heads. If they had a chance, that was it. He reached into his pocket and brought out his scout knife, thanking his guardian angel that he had acquired the habit of always carrying it. There was a screw driver blade. He unsnapped it, handed Scotty the light, and went to work.

The water was up to their ankles now, and rising fast. The first screw stuck. Rick took the knife in both hands and turned, and the screw driver blade gave a little. Sweat started out on his forehead. If the blade broke . . .

The screw gave and started to turn. Working as fast as he could he spun the knife, got the screw started well, then went to the next one. Scotty bent and finished removing the first screw with his fingers.

Two screws . . . three . . . and the water was up to their calves, almost at the bottom of the door. Four . . . the fifth stuck. Scotty rapped the metal under it with his pinch bar. Rick tried again, and it came free.

The sixth . . . and six to go.

The water reached the bottom of the circular steel plate, covered the lower screws.

"Hurry," Scotty pleaded.

Rick shifted to the lowest screws. Took one out, then another. The ninth stuck, too, and it was under water.

Scotty swung the pinch bar and water splashed. The screw held.

The water was rising fast. Most of the steel plate was covered now. Rick worked frantically, his hands under water. The screw refused to yield. He twisted hard, and the screw driver blade gave again. The water covered the steel plate entirely.

Rick was crouching low, only his shoulders above the water now. He skipped the stubborn screw and fumbled for the next one. Scotty held the light at the surface of the water and Rick's hands were green in the beam as he worked at the screw. It came free. Three to go, and one of them stuck!

The water was up to his neck as he crouched. He pressed his lips tightly together and went after the tenth. His wet hands slipped as he twisted, and the knife dropped!

Rick fell to his knees, groping for it. He found it, but precious seconds had been lost; the water was at his chin.

The screw gave. Two to go, including the one that was stuck.

He fumbled for the slot, twisted. The screw refused to yield. He took a deep breath and went back to work, his nose and mouth under the water. The screw held.

He straightened up, filled his lungs and went back at it. Gripping with both hands, he twisted. The screw gave slightly—and the knife fell apart in his hands!

Rick stood up, holding the knife in the light Scotty held. The rivets holding it together had given under the strain. With shaking fingers he pulled the knife completely apart and separated the screw driver blade from the others. Then he plunged back under the water and fumbled for the screw slot. It hurt his fingers cruelly, but he gritted his teeth and twisted. The screw gave. He turned it rapidly and pulled it loose.

Only the badly stuck one was left, and it would never give now with only the fragment of the knife for leverage.

But Scotty was moving into action. He reached down and found the rim of the steel plate, then, with his fingers, he pulled it loose enough to insert the pinch bar. He threw his weight on the bar and the plate came loose, pivoting down out of the way on the remaining screw.

Rick was under water instantly, his sensitive fingers probing in the lock's inner workings. He felt an oddly shaped wheel to which metal bars were fixed. His racing mind reconstructed the picture. The outer wheel turned the inner one, and the bars, which were pivoted on the inner wheel, slid the locking bolts into place. He grabbed the wheel, but his hands couldn't get a grip through the intervening locking bars, then he had to come up for air.

The water was above the door level, up to his shoulders when he stood up!

"The bar," he yelled, and took it from Scotty. "Hold me down!"

He went under, and Scotty's hands found his shoulders and forced him down.

It had to be now!

His searching fingers found the locking wheel and guided the pinch bar in. Then, braced against Scotty's hands, he pushed with all his strength. The wheel moved a fraction of an inch. He pushed again, and felt it give a little. The pressure of the bar was turning the wheel, withdrawing the locking bolts!

He kicked as a signal and Scotty let him up. He gasped for air in the rapidly filling chamber. The water was up to his chin, standing!

Filling his lungs, he went under again, found the place for the pinch bar and threw his weight against it, his legs driving. The wheel turned slowly. Rick kept the pressure on it, ignoring his burning lungs. Scotty pushed from above, holding him under, giving him leverage.

The bar was suddenly loose in his hands! He started to yell, then his mouth was full of water. He shot forward as though catapulted. There was an instant of chaos, then he was gasping clean, cool air. He staggered to his feet in time to see Scotty pile out of the fractionator in a surge of water.

Scotty took Rick's arm and squeezed it. "Boy, I thought we were a couple of drowned dumplings for sure."

Rick nodded weakly. The water stopped its turbulent rush as it spread over the ground. He looked around him and saw no one. Only the beat of the pump engine broke the silence.

The light was still working. Scotty flashed it around, and it came to rest on the fractionator panel. Aluminum gleamed dully through the black paint.

They walked to it, still unsteady. The control panel was a battered mass of twisted metal.

Scotty went back and searched until he found the

pinch bar. Water was still running out of the concrete box, but slowly now.

Silently they walked down to the pump house and shut the engine off. There was no sign of anyone in the plant grounds.

"They did a good job," Rick said bitterly.

"Almost too good," Scotty replied with a shudder.

"I can't figure out why they turned the pump on," Rick said. "They had us trapped. They could have wrecked everything without any trouble from us."

They stopped walking and stared at each other in the dim starlight.

"They must have deliberately set out to get us," Rick said, and the knowledge was an icy ball in the pit of his stomach.

CHAPTER IX

The Warning

TOM BLAKELY paced the floor of the Quonset hut, Doug straddled a chair and looked at the boys, who sat on one of the bunks. The young engineer's face was grave as he nodded agreement with what Tom was saying.

"All right, you say you looked the plant over thoroughly and nothing was damaged but the fractionator panel. Do you know what I think? Damaging the panel was an afterthought."

Doug started. "But that means . . ."

"Yes," Tom stated harshly. "This business tonight wasn't aimed at the plant at all. If damage had been all they were after, they wouldn't have turned on the pump. And they would have systematically ruined everything in sight."

He stopped pacing and faced the two boys.

"What do you know that makes you dangerous to anyone?"

Rick stared at him, wide-eyed. Scotty's jaw dropped. "Nothing," Rick replied. "What made you ask that?"

"It adds up," Tom said grimly. "This business tonight was an attempt on your lives. It wasn't intended to be anything else. I'm sure the wrecking of the panel was an afterthought. Well, if anyone wanted to get you out of the way, it can't be because of your value to the plant, otherwise they would have gone after Doug or me. So you must be dangerous because you know something. I can't think of any other reason."

"Neither can I," Doug agreed. "So I'm firing both of you. You're staying here tonight with us, and leaving for Spindrift first thing in the morning."

Rick found his voice. "But you can't send us away!"

"Oh, yes, we can," Tom said flatly. "We'd rather junk the whole plant than have you risk your lives by staying here. You're fired, and that's final!"

And despite the boys' protests, the partners were adamant.

"There may not even be jobs much longer," Tom pointed out. "If Carstairs refuses to give us the processing units, we'll have to fold, because we can't pay cash for them. Our investigation of the books tonight showed us that we're on thin ice. We can pay the workmen from Bridgeport for about a week's work."

"So turn in, both of you," Doug ordered. "Tom and I are going to stand guard the rest of the night."

Rick saw from the stubborn set of Doug's jaw that he

wasn't fooling. Both boys had gotten out of their wet clothes before the partners arrived and were wrapped in blankets.

"Okay," Scotty said resignedly.

Rick lay awake for a long while, thinking things over. He decided it would be best to return to Spindrift without argument. Then they would return on Monday, as though nothing had happened. He hoped that by then the plant would be humming with imported workmen and the partners would be too busy to worry.

There was something else . . . something about their being locked in the fractionator. He tried to puzzle out what it was that bothered him, but he was too tired to think clearly. Those long minutes working at the lock had taken plenty out of him. Out of Scotty, too, to judge by the deep breathing from the other bed. Rick turned on his side and bunched his pillow up comfortably, and went to sleep.

The boys awoke to full daylight and the appetizing aroma of bacon and eggs. Tom was playing chef. He greeted them cheerfully.

"Doug's out looking at the fractionator. Rise and shine and get this chow into you, then clear out. Your pay checks are on the desk."

The boys dressed quickly in clothes that were dry, but wrinkled and uncomfortable. By the time they had eaten, Doug had returned.

"The panel's a total loss," he reported, "but fortunately, I have the necessary parts to build it over again. I'll start on it right away."

"I suppose we'd better be going," Rick said meekly. "We'll have to go to the hotel and pick up our bags."

"Are you all right?" Tom asked. "Able to fly?"

"I'm right as a trivet." Rick grinned. "Whatever a trivet is. When will we see you again?"

"When the plant is operating," Doug answered. "We'll come to Spindrift, if we may."

"You'll always be welcome," Rick assured him.

They shook hands all around and the boys left. At the gate, they bumped into Tony, who looked at them sharply and growled a greeting.

"Seeing Tony reminded me," Rick said as they hiked into town. "I knew last night there was something queer about our being locked in. It was the pump. Remember how you couldn't start it and Tony had to?"

Scotty stopped short. "Gosh, yes! And I thought of something, too. Who knew that we'd be there alone? Tony!"

"But we don't have any evidence against Tony," Rick objected, remembering what Tom had said. "Anyone who knew something about engines could have started the pump. You could have, once you'd seen that the choke didn't work."

"Sure," Scotty agreed. "And Cunner or Lewis could have seen Tom and Doug leave the plant. They would have guessed we were alone."

They were silent for a moment, then Rick spoke up. "That's a whole lot of coincidence, though."

"I don't believe in coincidences," Scotty agreed, "but we have to have something more definite on Tony before we can accuse him."

"Anyway, we can keep an eye on him," Rick said. "And we can tell Doug and Tom what we suspect."

Cap'n Galt was at his desk when they returned to the lobby.

"Well," he exclaimed, "I'll be tarnal blamed if it ain't the two prodigal sons! And where were you last night?"

"We stayed at the plant," Rick said. "Cap'n, is Fred Lewis around?"

The old man's bright eyes narrowed. "Now, s'funny you should ask that. He checked out last night. Didn't say where he was goin'."

"Thanks," Scotty said grimly. "Well, good-bye, Cap'n. We'll see you on Monday."

"Don't know why you pay for a room," Cap'n Galt said tartly. "You don't use it none to speak of."

"It's a place to leave our clothes," Rick said, grinning. "So long, Cap'n."

"Funny Lewis should leave just then," Rick said, as they headed back toward the plant, "almost as though he wanted to get out of town before we were found in the fractionator."

"Maybe that's just why he checked out," Scotty said. "Do we stop in and say good-bye to the partners?"

"Sure."

As they approached the Quonset hut, they suddenly heard Tom's voice. He was almost yelling, and he sounded angry.

"Let them threaten! We'll get police protection and I'll carry a sawed-off shotgun if I have to. Tony can do the same."

The boys broke into a run. As they barged into the Quonset hut, the partners and Tony looked up.

"You're supposed to be on your way home," Tom said.

"We're going," Rick assured him. "What's up?"

"A message Tony found tacked on the fence a few minutes ago," Doug said. "We've called the police about it, and we're going to tell them about what happened to you last night. It's time we stopped trying to fight our battles alone."

Tom silently held up a placard on which was printed in bold letters:

IF YOU TRY TO IMPORT WORKERS THE OUTRAGED CITIZENS OF CRAYVILLE WILL FIGHT!

CHAPTER X

Cunner's Raid

It was with mixed feelings that Rick landed the Cub on the beach on Monday morning. He had assured Scotty that the partners would let them stay, because they would be so busy that they wouldn't have time to argue. Inwardly, he was not so sure.

And then, by returning to Crayville, they were walking into the enemy's territory again. If they knew the identity of the enemy, they could guard themselves. But who was he? They had talked over the problem a dozen times during the week end without coming to any satisfactory conclusion.

They hiked up to the road and walked briskly toward the plant. Rick wiped moist palms on his handkerchief. Tom and Doug couldn't make them leave; they had to be in at the finish.

Doug was leaning against the plant gate, and two burly guards were with him.

"And where do you think you're heading?" Doug asked.

"To work," Rick replied with more confidence than he felt.

"Not here. Listen, you beavers, haven't you any sense? You just climb back in that kite and get out of here. How do you think Tom and I would feel? We hate funerals."

"Aw, it's not that bad," Scotty said.

"No? Except for the minor miracle of Rick carrying a scout knife, you'd be needing a funeral. Don't forget that!"

"We'll be safe," Rick persisted. "We'll stick close to the plant, and we won't get into a corner. Please, Doug."

"How about the nighttime? Going to sit up all night with shotguns on your knees?"

"We'll be all right as long as there are people around," Scotty insisted.

"I suppose so," Doug said, "but there won't be people around after working hours and we haven't room to put you up in the hut."

Rick saw that the young engineer was weakening. "We'll go back to Spindrift at night," he suggested swiftly. "How about that?"

"I'll think about it," Doug said. "Anyway, you can come in and have breakfast with me." To the guards, he added: "You fellows can knock off now. I'll see you to-night."

In the Quonset hut, he grinned at them. "Tom will break my neck, but I have to admit it's nice having you around. If you go home at night I suppose it will be all right."

"We will," Scotty assured him. "Gosh, Doug, thanks. I was sure you wouldn't even let us in the place. Where's Tom?"

"He and Tony went to Bridgeport to pick up the men. We rented a couple of trucks. They should be here soon."

Rick took a seat on a bunk. "Anything exciting happen over the week end?"

"Nothing much. We rechecked the pump last night, and I got the fractionator panel rebuilt. If everything goes smoothly from now on, we may make out. By the way, Carstairs agreed to let us have the fractionators Friday afternoon. We had to sign a demand note, but we figured that was all right."

"What's a demand note?" Scotty asked.

"Payable on demand. Our other notes were dated ahead, but this one comes due when they ask for the money. They're just protecting themselves, I suppose. Still . . ."

"Did you call the police?" Rick asked.

"Yes. They're standing by to escort the trucks here."

"Tell Doug about Tony," Scotty said.

"What about Tony?" Doug asked quickly.

Rick outlined their suspicions, mentioning the difficulty of starting the engine and adding that apparently only Tony knew they would be alone at the plant that night. "Of course we haven't any proof, but it looks queer," he finished. "What do you know about Tony, anyway?"

"Not much," Doug agreed. "Still, he's worked hard for us and I'd hate to believe he'd have any part in a thing like that."

"Don't say anything to him," Rick suggested. "We'll all keep an eye on him."

Doug nodded, then stood up as the sound of a truck engine broke the stillness outside the hut. "They must be coming now."

They reached the gate just as the truck driven by Tom turned in, escorted by a State Police trooper on a motorcycle.

"Not a bit of trouble," the trooper called. "But we'll take no chances. A couple of men will meet your trucks tonight, at five."

Doug thanked him, and he rode off as the other truck came through the gate, driven by Tony. Tom parked his truck and got out. He started with surprise as he saw the two boys.

Rick caught sight of a big, blond worker leaping from the truck and he grabbed Scotty's arm.

"Listen! Isn't that the big guy we saw in Zukky's that first day we landed?"

Scotty moved past a few workmen for a clearer look.

"The same one," he agreed. "Say, do you think . . ."

"We'd better find out," Rick said. He took Doug aside and rapidly told him of seeing the big man at the restaurant where they had first seen Cunner.

Doug beckoned to Tom and the four of them faced the big man. He was not very old, and built like an athlete. Under his jacket he wore the same red shirt the boys remembered.

"We've seen you before," Rick stated. "In Zukky's, a couple of Sundays ago."

White teeth flashed in an engaging grin. "Ho! You gotta good mem'ries, I think. You remember Mike Kozac, hey? Well. Mike he remember you, too. You almost have fight with that fat man, hey?"

"What were you doing in Crayville?" Scotty demanded.

"Where do you live?" Tom's question followed at once.

The big man's candid blue eyes were puzzled. "I gotta gal in Crayville. I come here maybe two, three times a week. Me, I live in Bridgeport, and the employ' man, he say who wants work Crayville, so I think by golly I take this job and maybe see my Carlotta. She's a nice gal, that Carlotta. Maybe so we get married, I like this job. We see."

"Sounds reasonable," Doug said.

Rick liked the blond giant's looks. He had a wide, friendly grin, and he didn't look as though he were capable of doing anyone a meanness. "I think he's okay," he agreed.

"I think you okay, too," Mike Kozac said amiably. "Well, why we wait? Where's this work we do, hey?"

"Tony!" Doug called. "Let's get going. Take ten of these men and start the new foundations for the pressure domes. I've marked them out. You know what's wanted. Now, which of you men are carpenters? We asked for ten."

A group of men stepped forward.

"Got your tools? In the trucks? Okay, get them and come with me."

Doug inspected the remaining twenty men, then beckoned to Kozac.

"Kozac, I'm making you a straw boss. We want this fence torn down and the boards stacked over by those tanks. Don't damage the lumber any more than you can help. You'll find pinch bars, crowbars, and hammers in the Quonset hut. Think you can handle it?"

Kozac's grin flashed. "Is a lead peep cinch. Come on, you strong guys, tearing down is more easy than build'."

Things began to hum. The boys found themselves abandoned and had to hurry after Doug for instructions. He got the carpenters started on building the chemical platforms and roofing over the sediment tanks, then led the boys to a corner of the Quonset hut where a number of boxes were stacked.

"These are the chemical nozzles. You'll find them packed in cosmoline. They'll have to be cleaned.

"Cosmoline," Scotty groaned. "I thought I was through with that when I got out of the Marines!"

"What is it?" Rick asked.

"Preservative. Gummy as tar and stubborn as glue. We'll have to use gasoline."

Rick found out that Scotty hadn't exaggerated. Cleaning the nozzles was a messy, aggravating job. The gasoline fumes made his head ache. He suggested taking the job out of doors and Scotty readily agreed.

Outside, they found the fence vanishing at a miraculous rate. Already one full side, the one toward town, was gone, uprights and all. It looked strange to see the town across the fields of bunch grass and scrub growth. The carpenters were working rapidly, too. They had one platform partially completed. A second group was putting up the uprights that would support the roof over the tank. Two men did nothing but examine the boards that Mike's men brought, take out the nails, select those to be used, and pass them up to the other carpenters.

Tom came and scowled at them.

"So Doug softened up, did he? But don't think you're getting away with anything. I'll have my eye on you." He winked and went into the hut. They heard him humming as he began his paper work.

"A great pair," Rick said.

"Yes." Scotty agreed. "Swell guys, both of them. Listen, are we actually going home tonight?"

"Guess we'll have to. Besides, it's probably the smart thing to do."

They were quiet for a time as they worked at the brown, gummy preservative. The pile of clean, shining nozzles was growing; they were making progress.

"Funny the fishermen didn't try to interfere with the trucks," Scotty said at last.

"Maybe they didn't want to buck the police," Rick replied absently.

"Could be. But, say, how would they know the police would be there?" Scotty asked, puzzled.

That hadn't occurred to Rick. He thought it over. "Well, maybe they didn't. Maybe it was a bluff."

"If it was, Cunner fell down on the job. Maybe Tony tipped them off."

"Gosh, that's right," Rick said. "If Tony—"

"Watch it!" Scotty warned, and pointed.

The fence in front of the plant was vanishing board by board. Mike Kozac was walking over toward them from where his crew was working.

"Pretty fast, hey?" he grinned. "Mike Kozac is one good worker, like I told you."

"We believe it," Rick said.

Mike sat down and mopped his face. "This is funny place. What they make here, hey?"

"All kinds of things."

The big man pointed toward the secret vault. "What's in there? Maybe money?"

"Maybe," Rick answered shortly.

"You'll have to ask the boss," Scotty said.

"I ask already." Mike yawned. "He don't know, too."

The boys laughed as he went back to his gang.

"That's some accent," Rick remarked. "What is it? Slav? French?"

Scotty grinned. "A little of everything."

Tom came out of the hut, consulting his watch. "Knock off, you beavers. It's time for chow. Pass the word, will you?"

It didn't seem possible that the morning had gone so fast, but Rick's appetite told him that it had. He and Scotty ran to the various working groups, passing the word that it was noontime.

Doug looked displeased. "Well," he said, "if we have to eat, I suppose we just have to. Okay, fellows. Break out the lunches."

He walked back to the hut with the boys. "I hate to take time out even to eat. Oh, well, I shouldn't complain. Everything's going like clockwork. You hungry?"

Rick grinned. "Scotty is."

"And you're not, of course. No hungrier than a starving wolf," Scotty said derisively.

"We'll break out that can of beans I've been saving," Doug suggested. "Bean sandwiches. Best indigestion breeders I ever invented."

Tom had already put the coffee pot on and was opening the beans. Bread and butter, and a can of pickles were on the table.

"If the goblins don't get you, the chow will," Doug said cheerfully.

Outside, the workmen were sitting down to the lunches they had brought. They were a good-natured crew, Rick thought. They seemed to take their cue from big Mike Kozac.

"Start making sandwiches," Tom invited. "If you're really hungry, you'll find cold meat in the icebox."

"That's more like it," Doug exclaimed.

A voice outside the door demanded, "Where's them two boys? The young ones?"

Rick started. "Listen, that's Cap'n Galt!"

He hurried to the door and called, "In here, Cap'n."

The old man looked hot and uncomfortable. He pulled open the screen door and glared at them. "Well, what you waitin' on? Ain't you goin' to fight?"

"Fight?" Tom spoke past a mouthful of sandwich. "Fight whom?"

"I reckon I knowed you wouldn't be awake," the Cap'n snorted. "The fishermen, that's who! They're gettin' worked up down at Zukky's, and they'll be here afore long, Cunner leadin' 'em. And they're mad, I'll tell a man! Killin' mad. On account of the oyster beds has been poisoned!"

Rick spoke out of the stunned silence. "Cap'n, are you sure?"

"Sure? Sure I'm sure! Now don't say you ain't been warned." Cap'n Galt turned and stomped out.

Doug jumped into action. Picking up the phone, he demanded State Police headquarters. The connection took only a minute. He explained rapidly what was coming and asked for aid.

"Be there within fifteen minutes," the police officer said.

"That's that," Doug said as he hung up. He went to the door and called, "Tony! Get the workmen up here, and hurry it up!"

Tom hurried out, calling back, "I'll keep an eye open up the road."

"How did they find out the oyster beds were poisoned?" Scotty demanded. "There's no 'r' in June. Oysters aren't in season."

"That business of oysters not being in season when there's no 'r' in the month doesn't mean anything on the coast," Rick said. "People around here eat oysters any time. Anyway, the only reason that stuff was started about not eating oysters during the summer months was because they spoiled in the heat. We have refrigeration nowadays." He broke off and pointed. "Here come the workmen."

The workers gathered before the Quonset hut, waiting curiously for what Doug had to say. When they were all clustered around, he spoke to them.

"Men, we've just had word that the Crayville fishermen are coming to wreck the plant. They claim the oyster beds have been poisoned. Perhaps they have, but certainly not by us. If you stay here, it means a fight, probably a tough one. I'd like to offer you bonuses to stay and fight, but the plant just hasn't the money. Whatever you decide to do will be all right."

The men were quiet for a moment, looking at each other as though in silent question, then Mike Kozac stepped forward.

"Mr. Boss," he said quietly, "no one runs Mike Kozac off a job. I don't care how many fishers is coming. They come; they find Mike. And I have a big club in my hand, you bet."

A carpenter stepped to Mike's side. "He's talking for me, too. I'm sticking."

Rick glanced at Tony. The foreman was watching, his face impassive.

The other workers stepped forward, too, all talking at once. They agreed with Mike. No one was running them off their new jobs!

Only Tony hung back. Doug Chambers called out, "How about you, Tony?"

The foreman shook his head. "You pay me to work, not to fight. I want no part of it."

Scotty took a half step toward him, and Rick saw his

friend's dislike of the dark man coming to the surface.

"Timid, Tony?" he asked. "Or don't you want to fight your friends?"

The foreman's hands came up. "You don't talk to me like that, kid! I'll beat your ears down!"

"Start beating," Scotty said cheerfully.

Doug stepped between them. "That's enough. Tony, it's your privilege to decide for yourself. But if our only old hand runs off while the new men stay, I don't think that leaves me much choice. I'll make out your check right now."

The workers scattered as Tony and Doug went into the hut. Rick saw them hefting pieces of two by four. Some of them picked up the steel pinch bars with which they had torn down the fence.

"Better find something to swing with," Scotty advised. "Those fishermen won't be using powder puffs." He found a club and handed it to Rick. "I'll use this," he said, unbuckling his belt. Scotty always wore a Marine belt with a heavy brass buckle. Now he wound it around his hand, leaving the buckle hanging free. It made a lethal weapon.

Scotty gave Rick a strained grin. "I'm not swinging, except in self-defense. We have to remember that these fishermen have been lied to and stirred up. They're acting honestly, according to their way of thinking."

"My sentiments exactly," Doug said from behind them.

Rick turned and saw Tony leaving the plant, cutting across the field. Good riddance, he thought.

Doug hailed the workmen, and they crowded around. They were all armed.

"We want no trouble," Doug said. "If they want a fight, let them start it. And try not to get too rough. We're only defending our property. We want no unnecessary violence."

Tom arrived out of breath.

"They're coming," he said. "Down the road. There must be fifty of them. And Cunner Stoles is in the lead. I recognized him from Rick's description."

The body of workmen moved toward what had been the front gate of the plant, Doug, Tom, and the boys in the lead. Glancing up the road, Rick saw a phalanx of roughly dressed men walking slowly toward them. They were carrying what appeared to be baseball bats.

Both groups were silent as the fishermen advanced, and then the marching gang of townsmen reached the plant and the two bodies of men faced each other.

Cunner Stoles, his face redder than ever, a wicked-looking billy in his hand, stepped forward.

"Your plant's going to get wrecked," he stated. "We don't want to hurt anyone, but we're aimin' to break up this thing once and for all. You poisoned our oyster beds and ruined the living of some of us. The oysters are all green, and they're dyin'. So step aside. We're comin' in."

"Not so fast!" Doug stepped forward to meet him. "We didn't poison the beds. We haven't even been operating."

"We heard your pump last night. We know you're lyin'."

Behind Cunner, the fishermen growled angrily.

Mike Kozac came out of the group of plant workmen. "It's you who lies, Cunner," he said flatly. "You been pumpin' these men full of lies for weeks. I heard you. This plant don't poison nothin'. And what you care about oyster beds? You cheap, rotting, good for nuttin'! You never do a day's good work long as you live."

Rick took a deep breath. Cunner's face was scarlet, the veins standing out on it.

"Don't you say that to me!"

"I say it," Mike said. "I mean it." He addressed the fishermen. "You honest men. You work. Why you listen to this Cunner? You a bunch of fools? When he ever tell the truth, I ask you? Not once! You believe him now? Ha! You are stupids."

There was a low murmur from the fishermen. For a moment Rick felt hopeful. Mike's words made sense to them. Give them time to think . . .

But Cunner didn't. With a wild yell he flung himself on Mike Kozac.

Mike's big fist lifted and caught Cunner squarely on the chin, lifting him bodily, throwing him back into the ranks of fishermen. But the Crayville men were already charging forward; the possibility of peace had vanished with Cunner's act.

For a heartbeat the press of men held Cunner Stoles upright, then they surged by and he fell face down in the road. When Big Mike hit anyone, they stayed hit.

The two groups surged toward each other yelling. For a moment Rick stood hesitant, then a fisherman jumped at him, club raised. All around him there was the shock of man meeting man, club meeting club.

The fight to save the sea mine plant was on!

CHAPTER XI

The Car with the Broken Bumper

RICK side-stepped the blow aimed at him by the fisherman and the club whizzed harmlessly by. He lifted his own stick, but the fishermen suddenly hesitated and backed up. Then, amazingly, he threw down his weapon and stalked off.

For an instant Rick was puzzled, then he realized that Mike Kozac's words hadn't fallen on barren soil. They had taken much of the anger out of the Crayville men. He turned and saw Scotty engaged in a duel with a burly fisherman. His friend was parrying halfhearted swings of a long club.

Down near the Quonset hut, however, a vicious fight was raging. Doug was in the thick of it, warding off blows from three fisherman. Rick saw Mike Kozac sprint to the engineer's rescue and started for the fight himself, running past Scotty and his assailant. Then a terrible wave of sound engulfed him, froze him in his tracks.

BAROOM!

The fishermen and workmen halted in mid-swing and stood like a horrified tableau for a fraction of a second, then they were all running toward the sound of the explosion. Rick saw smoke billowing from one of the sediment tanks and rushed toward the spot.

"Grenades!" Scotty yelled.

BAROOOOOOM!

The concussion jarred Rick, almost knocked him down. He staggered, then recovered his balance and streaked toward the sediment tanks. Scotty came up almost abreast of him, his legs driving like pistons.

Smoke blanketed the tanks now, and a workman staggered out of the veil and fell headlong. Rick turned to help him, and from the corner of his eye he saw two running figures crossing the field next to the plant. Then noting that Scotty was almost at the fallen workman's side, Rick turned again toward the field and the two sprinting men.

He recognized them instantly: Fred Lewis! There was no mistaking that black suit and gray hat. The other was Tony Larzo. Rick sprang after them.

They reached the road while Rick was still far behind. He saw Lewis run down the highway toward town, saw Tony dash across it into the brush on the other side.

They were the grenade throwers, he was sure of it!

For an instant Rick hesitated, unsure of which one to follow, then he kept going after Fred Lewis. Tony was only a hireling; perhaps Lewis was the boss. He had to stay with him. If someone had actually seen the grenades thrown, they had Lewis cold!

Rick reached the road and saw the black-suited figure a hundred yards ahead, still running all out. The boy increased his stride, arms and legs pumping as he tried to catch up. Lewis swerved into a patch of woods, and Rick ran off the road, intent on cutting him off.

A car engine roared. Through the trees he saw a black sedan spurt forward, reach the road, and turn toward town. He let out a yell of frustrated anger. Lewis was getting away!

The black sedan's tires screamed on the pavement as it turned the corner onto the road and then it was gone, leaving him standing helplessly, staring after it. He caught a glimpse of a yellow license plate and knew that it was a New York car, but the sedan had gone too fast to give him time to get the license number. He had also noticed that the bumper was hanging on one side as though it had caught on something and pulled free.

He certainly couldn't follow the car on foot. Then inspiration struck him. The Cub!

He turned and ran back, angling toward the water front. He reached the plant, running hard, and looked around for Scotty. Workmen and fishermen were gathered at the sediment tanks. He let out a yell, but no one looked up; they were too occupied with the bombed tanks. He didn't have time to turn aside. He kept going, running down the beach toward the plane.

In a moment the ropes that tied the Cub to driftwood logs were free and the warning device disconnected. He advanced the throttle and turned on the switch, then ran around front and swung the propeller through. The well-kept engine caught at once. He jumped in and jazzed the throttle, an anxious eye on his engine temperature. For a moment he waited, giving the engine a chance to warm, then he taxied to the end of the strip, kicked the tail around and pushed the throttle far forward, holding the plane on the brakes.

The tail came up under the propeller blast and he released the brakes, silently praying. The engine coughed once and his heart almost stopped, but the little plane responded, leaping into the air in a full-stall take-off. In a moment he was climbing, parallel with the beach. He thought he saw Scotty run out of the group around the sediment tanks and wave, but he wasn't sure. Then he settled down to the business of finding the black sedan.

He swept low over the town, watching the roads; there was no sign of the quarry there. He banked around and followed the road that led out of town toward Milford. In a moment he picked up the black sedan, racing along the highway. And, coming from the other direction, he saw two State Police cruisers, heading at top speed for the plant.

A little late, Rick thought bitterly. But it wasn't their fault. Not ten minutes had elapsed since Doug had phoned, although it seemed like half a day. He glanced at his watch. It was 12:11.

He banked in lazy circles, always keeping behind the fleeing sedan, and tried to reconstruct what had happened. The fight must have been staged as a cover-up, just to make an opportunity for Tony and Lewis to bomb the plant. That had to be the answer.

He shook his head over Tony's defection, but it provided a lot of answers. All the "accidents" at the plant had undoubtedly been his doing. He could even have adulterated the cement for the pressure domes. It was likely that he had. And no one had suspected him. It seemed certain now that Tony had been one of the men who locked them in the fractionator.

The Milford turnoff was just ahead. Rick watched the sedan speeding along the black ribbon of road toward the fork ahead and waited for it to make the turn. But the intersection passed and the sedan kept on going. He knew then that Lewis was making for the Merritt Parkway.

The Cub whirled in lazy circles, always behind the sedan so that Lewis couldn't see it. Rick hoped he would stop somewhere, giving a chance to put the Cub down and phone for help. Once Lewis got on the Merritt Parkway, the chance would be gone. He could lose the Cub by turning off at any of the towns en route, vanishing from sight in the maze of city traffic.

The black sedan seemed to crawl toward the parkway entrance, but Rick knew it was going very fast. He watched closely as the car edged onto the concrete parkway and picked up speed again, heading south!

If Lewis turned off at Bridgeport, there would be no chance of following him. He had to get a car or lose his quarry.

Rick made an instant decision and swung south, turning seaward to pick up Steve's airport. There was another entrance to the parkway near the airport. He could borrow a car and wait at the entrance until Lewis passed. He gave the little plane all the throttle it would take and left Lewis far behind. In a few moments he was losing altitude to come in for a landing. The ground came up and the wheels touched in a tail-high landing. He kept flying speed as he made a wide turn for the hangar, not letting the tail drop until he was almost at the door. Then he killed the engine and braked to a stop right before the gas pumps. He was out of the plane before it stopped rolling.

Steve Hollis came out of the hangar wiping his hands on a bit of waste.

"Rick! What the heck kind of a landing was that? That ain't the way I taught you."

"Listen, Steve, I've got to have a car. Lend me yours, will you? It's important. I can't explain now, only I'm chasing someone."

Steve's calm eyes gauged the measure of Rick's excitement, then he nodded. "Take the coupé. The keys are in it. And for the sake of my needy family, bring it back in one piece, will you?"

"I'll be careful," Rick called over his shoulder. "Will you take care of the Cub?"

"Roger."

He noted as he started the coupé that the tank was full. That was good; he wouldn't be delayed by having to stop for gas. He shifted and shot the car across the apron and turned onto the highway. A half mile up the road he took the turn that led to the Merritt Parkway.

The black sedan was somewhere between the Crayville entrance to the parkway and the one he would take. There were no exits in that stretch where Lewis could turn off. Rick planned his strategy. With any kind of luck he could stay with the black sedan until Lewis reached a destination. He couldn't guess what would happen then, but he could hope for a break!

He drove the coupé onto the twisting ramp that led to the parkway, then pulled over to the side, well back from the actual entrance. Now to wait until the black sedan passed. Rick was sure Lewis wouldn't suspect he was being trailed. He probably had watched the road behind him from Crayville to the parkway, and he had seen nothing. He wouldn't be suspicious.

Cars whipped by as Rick waited. He kept close watch of the southbound traffic until he saw the black sedan with the broken bumper. He caught a glimpse of Lewis's white face, then he moved into the stream of traffic and settled down to the chase.

As they approached the Bridgeport turnoff, he closed the distance until his was the second car behind Lewis, but the man with the white face shot right on by. Rick guessed now that he was heading for New York.

The Merritt Parkway ended after an hour's drive, and the Hutchinson River Parkway began, with no perceptible change except for the sign that said they were now in New York State.

Rick settled down to a long drive. Lewis was keeping within the speed limit.

The minutes and miles passed and New York City drew closer. Lewis went by the Long Island turnoff without even slowing. Definitely now, he was bound for some point in New York. The chase sped through Westchester County and into the Bronx, then onto the Henry Hudson Parkway that leads into the West Side Express Highway.

Lewis led the way right down the length of midtown Manhattan. Rick kept a shorter distance now, because there were ramps leading down to the city every few blocks, but not until they approached Twenty-fourth Street did the quarry show signs of leaving the elevated highway. Rick pulled up until only one car separated them.

The black sedan shot down the next exit ramp, Rick

close behind. They stopped for the traffic light and Rick let a delivery truck get between them. They must be nearing the end of the trail.

Lewis stayed under the elevated highway until he reached Fourteenth Street. then he went across the avenue, heading east. Rick stayed close and saw his quarry turn down Eighth Avenue, go a couple of blocks down the avenue, then suddenly swing into a garage.

Rick shot right by, turned into the next street and stopped in a convenient parking space. He got out and ran back around the corner, fearful that he had lost Lewis. If there were several entrances to the garage, he was sunk. He crossed the avenue, keeping an eye on the main entrance, and took up his station at the corner.

For perhaps five minutes he watched with growing anxiety, then he saw Lewis come out and walk briskly uptown. There weren't too many people on the streets right then, so Rick remained on the opposite side of the avenue. At Fourteenth, Lewis crossed over toward him and he ducked into a doorway. Lewis, still walking briskly, headed east.

There were more people now. Rick closed the distance, afraid of losing Lewis in the crowd. At the next corner, Lewis went into a cigar store. Rick peered in cautiously and saw him in a phone booth. He would have given much to hear that conversation, but he didn't dare try to get closer.

Presently Lewis came out, only to go into a subway

kiosk. Rick hurried after him, fishing for a nickel. He didn't have one. He shoved a half dollar at the man in the booth and got ten nickels back. He dropped one in the turnstile and hurried after the white-faced man. Lewis led the way through the underground passage to the uptown side, then waited on the express platform.

Rick watched from the shelter of a steel pillar.

It was easy to follow now. When Lewis got into a subway car, Rick got in the other end. When Lewis got off at Times Square, Rick followed, keeping a few people between him and Lewis.

Lewis strolled uptown, taking his time. Rick sauntered along fifty yards behind him. He wished he dared duck into a booth and call the plant, but he would lose the trail. He wished, too, that he had stopped to pick up Scotty; there would have been plenty of time, as things turned out, but he hadn't dared, then.

The trail led down Forty-ninth Street toward Sixth Avenue, and Rick saw the high bulk of Radio City just ahead. Were they heading there? He began to think so as they neared Sixth, but suddenly Lewis turned aside and vanished!

Rick broke into a run, then pulled up short as he saw why Lewis had seemed to disappear. He had gone into a basement restaurant, down a flight of stairs and through a door that was still gently swinging.

He drew back and peered through the windows. He saw the black-suited figure go down the left aisle. He saw a man rise to greet him. They shook hands and Lewis joined the man in the booth.

"I've got to get closer," Rick muttered to himself. He had to get a look at the man Lewis had met; he had to hear that conversation!

He examined the restaurant closely. It was rectangular, booths lining the walls on both sides. There was a double row of booths in the center, separated by a partition on which potted plants were set. Lewis and his friend were sitting in a booth halfway down, on the left side of the partition. The booth across the partition was empty.

Rick took his nerve in both hands and walked down the four stairs to the restaurant door.

CHAPTER XII

The Manila Envelope

RICK had seen that Lewis was sitting with his back to the door. He took out his handkerchief and held it to his nose in an attempt to hide his face in case the two men in the booth looked up. Then he went down the aisle to the right, and, crouching low, slid into the booth across the partition from them.

Not until he was seated, his head concealed by the row of potted plants, did he breathe freely again. Then he slid closer to the partition and took stock of his surroundings.

The partition that separated him from the two men came up to about eye level. On top of it were the plants, an effective screen. Rick saw that the walls on both sides were set with tall mirrors. By looking up, across the potted plants into the mirror on the opposite side, he could get a good view of the two men. It worked both ways, of course. If they looked over his head at the mirror on his side, they would see him.

140

But they were busy, intent on their conversation. Rick strained to hear what they were saying.

"What would you like?"

Rick almost jumped out of his skin before he realized it was only the waitress. He gave her a shaky smile. "Milk and a ham sandwich, please."

The mirror showed him that Lewis's companion was a man slightly past middle age, well dressed, and with a look that Rick thought of as well fed. Not fat, exactly, but inclined to pudginess. His face was clean-shaven, and pink, as though he had just come from the barber. Everything about him indicated wealth and self-confidence. His voice was rather high, but with a commanding timber.

"And then what?" he asked.

"Well, Tony met me in the field and I gave him the grenades. He knew just where to throw them. He made two direct hits. They won't be using those tanks again."

"Good. We'll give them a few days, then I'll issue instructions to take over. You've done well, my friend. Now, how about your men?"

"Tony is all right. We can trust him, and I've paid him well. But I'm not so sure about Stoles. He's a weakling. If they put the pressure on, he may talk."

"What do you intend to do about it?"

"I'll take care of him, never fear."

The waitress placed the sandwich and milk before Rick. He handed her a dollar bill, not wanting to bother fishing for change.

"You seem to be very good at that sort of thing," the stranger chuckled.

"Thanks. Now, how about that . . . you know."

Rick accepted the change and thrust it into his pocket. He gulped the milk, not taking his eyes from the mirror across the top of the plants.

The stranger chuckled again. "I keep my word," he said. "I promised you your passport to freedom if you came through for me. You shall have it. And that job is yours as soon as I complete arrangements."

Rick saw the stranger take a brief case from the seat next to him. He opened it and produced a large Manila envelope. Then he took out what seemed to be photographic prints and negatives and leafed through them, chuckling softly to himself.

"It was a good day for me when I got hold of these," he said. "They've kept you faithful, my friend."

"Give them to me." Lewis's voice was low and intense.

"Of course." The stranger stuffed them back into the envelope and pushed it across the table. "You see, I've included the negatives. Evidence of my good faith, my friend."

Rick had strained to see the contents of the envelope, but it was impossible. He thought: If I could get my hands on it . . .

It must be important; it must be evidence of the whole plot. Otherwise, how could the stranger have held it over Lewis's head, to force him to obey? For an instant he thought of snatching it, but they would be on him in a second. He pushed close to the partition, and the change in his pocket tinkled.

Inspiration struck him. If he could divert their attention . . . he had to get that envelope! He had to!

His glance went swiftly around, searching for an idea . . . he found it, under the table. The partition stopped within six inches of the floor. By bending low, he could see the feet of the men in the next booth. Lewis was moving his feet as though getting ready to leave. It had to be now or never!

Rick took a handful of change from his pocket. He bent low, and flung the coins under the partition! They rolled and clanged on the hard floor with a noise that made everyone look up.

In the mirror he saw the two men lean out toward the aisle, and he jumped up, reached across the partition and scooped up the envelope. Then, with fear and excitement giving wings to his heels, he sprinted for the door!

He gained the street and hesitated, not sure of which way to run, then he turned west and ran back the way he had come. As he ran, he tucked the envelope into his belt and buttoned his jacket over it. It was too big to fit into a pocket. Then he threw a glance back over his shoulder and saw Lewis emerge from the restaurant and stand irresolute.

Rick slowed to a sedate walk, knowing that a run would attract the man's attention. After a moment he looked back, and inhaled sharply. He had been seen! He broke into a run again, dodging the people on the street. Some stared curiously at him, but most paid little attention. Then, as he neared Seventh Avenue, the crowd grew thicker, slowing him down. He looked back frantically and saw Lewis pounding along behind him.

Rick tried the street, but cars forced him back to the crowded sidewalk again. He pushed through the crowd as fast as he could, and reached the corner of the avenue. The light was against him, but he jumped into the street anyway. A taxi whizzed by, almost brushing him. He leaped nimbly in front of a bus and had to stop short for another taxi. For a few terrible moments he was stranded between the traffic lanes, then a car slowed and he gained the opposite curb. When he looked back, Lewis was caught in the middle of the street, as he had been.

Rick sprinted toward Broadway, dodging in and out of the crowd. He had to lose Lewis!

He gained the corner of Broadway and looked back, to see Lewis reach the curb at Seventh and start up the short block. Rick crossed Forty-ninth Street to the north corner. Keep going west, he thought. He might be able to lose Lewis in the alleys west of Broadway. He started across against the light, and a brawny arm shoved him back.

"Cross on the light only, me boy!"

Rick glared at the policeman and turned up Broadway, the crowds slowing him down. In front of a theater he got hopelessly tangled with people who wouldn't let him past. He pushed through somehow, cold sweat starting out on his face. He glanced over his shoulder and saw Lewis. He saw the dark eyes in the white face and read murder in them.

The light was still against him, but he dodged in and out of traffic and reached the far side of Broadway. He was worried now. His superior speed meant nothing on the crowded streets, and if he pushed ahead too fast, there was always the possibility that a policeman might grab him. His racing thoughts searched for a way out, and his eyes came to rest on a subway kiosk.

If only a train came in at the right moment . . .

He turned the corner of Fiftieth Street and was held up for a moment when he tried to go down the exit, then he saw his mistake and ran to the entrance. Running now was all right. People would think he was running for a train.

He went down the long stairs as though he had wings, fishing for a nickel. Then he remembered. He had thrown all his coins away. He found a bill and thrust it through the wicket, breathing hard, half-turned to watch the stairs. The agent took his time about it. But at last Rick scooped up the change and ran to the turnstile. He put a coin in and pushed through onto the platform, then looked around for a passage to the other side of the tracks.

He ran to the far end of the platform, looking up the tracks anxiously for a sign of a train. The tracks were gleaming, empty ribbons of steel.

There was none! This was a local station with only one platform. He had trapped himself!

He was at the southern end of the platform. He put his back against the tiled wall and waited, hoping. If a train came before Lewis did, he would be all right. Perhaps Lewis had lost him. He might not have seen . . .

Lewis pushed through the turnstile.

Rick could only wait. He couldn't even seem to turn away. The unhurrying air of the man with the white face had an inevitability to it, as though he knew that the end was near.

Lewis surveyed the platform. He looked north, taking his time. He looked at the people close to him. He looked south. His piercing dark eyes met Rick's anguished ones.

The white face seemed to blur before Rick's eyes. He saw it move toward him, slowly, inevitably. He saw Lewis rub his hands in satisfaction. There was only fifty feet between them . . . forty . . . thirty . . .

With a strangled yell Rick threw off the hypnosis that had gripped him. He jumped from the platform, fell, narrowly missed the lethal third rail. He scrambled to his feet and ran downtown along the tracks. And, as he ran, he sensed the thrumming of the rails, heard sudden sound fill the tunnel.

A train was coming!

CHAPTER XIII

Scotty Takes a Hand

SCOTTY was sparring with his fisherman opponent when the explosion came. Instantly, their private war forgotten, they were racing side by side toward the noise.

"Grenade!" Scotty yelled. There was no mistaking the sound; he had heard it often enough during the war. He had thrown plenty of them himself.

The fisherman racing at his side gasped, "We had nothing to do with this, honest!"

Scotty saw Rick running, too, then the second explosion came and he lost sight of him.

The grenades had landed in two of the big sediment tanks, leaving them torn, twisted, and shrouded in smoke. He had a moment's thought that this would be the finish of the sea mine plant, then that was forgotten as a workman staggered out of the smoke and fell.

Scotty raced to his side and turned him over. A wet red stain was spreading on the man's shoulder. He ripped the shirt away and called to the fisherman who had been his opponent. "There's a first-aid kit in the Quonset hut. Get it! Lively, now. And have someone call a doctor."

He bent to the work of stanching the wound and examining the man for further damage. The shrapnel hole in his shoulder seemed to be all, but it was enough. Scotty's expert fingers probed until he was satisfied that no bones had been broken.

The fisherman arrived with the kit and the others began to crowd around. Doug pushed through and asked, "How bad is it?"

"He'll be all right," Scotty said. He selected tincture of merthiolate and swabbed the wound area, then he applied a compress and bandaged it into place. The doctor would have to probe for the shrapnel. "Go to the Quonset hut and bring one of the cots out here," he directed. "We'll use it as a stretcher."

"We had nothing to do with this," one of the fishermen proclaimed. "We want you guys to know that. We found the beds poisoned, and we were sore, but we wouldn't do anything like this."

The other fishermen nodded their agreement.

"I'm sure of it," Doug said.

"You were misinformed," Tom told them. "Cunner Stoles lied. There will be no poisonous wastes from this plant."

There was a yell from down near the water front, but

at that moment the wounded man groaned with return-ing consciousness and Scotty didn't look up.

"You'll be all right," he assured him. "It's just a little hole in your shoulder."

Two workmen arrived with a cot and Scotty directed three others to kneel, showing them how to lift the wounded man. In a moment he was comfortably settled on the cot and beginning to take an interest in his sur-roundings.

"What happened?" he asked.

Tom started to tell him. Just then Scotty heard the Cub engine catch. Rick! What was he doing in the Cub? He moved to the outer circle of men, listening. Some-thing was up, that was sure. Then the plane shot into sight and he gasped. Rick was in a hurry, to make a take-off like that! He ran out into the open and waved, but the plane shot overhead in the direction of Cray-ville.

"That was Rick," he said worriedly as Doug joined him. "What do you suppose he's up to?"

"I don't know," Doug replied. "But don't worry about him; he knows what he's doing."

"I hope," Scotty said.

Tom came up. "Who threw those bombs?" he asked.

None of them knew. They asked the question again, of the workmen. One thought he had seen two men in the field next to the plant, but in the confusion and noise he couldn't be sure.

"It wasn't any of us," a fisherman said.

"No," Doug replied grimly. "I'm sure of that. But you men have been used as dupes. This fight was staged just to give the bomb throwers a chance. I'm certain of it!"

The words made good sense to Scotty. "Then Cunner can give us some information," he said quickly. "He started the fight, remember?" He ran toward the road where he had seen Cunner fall after Mike Kozac hit him. The pudgy fisherman had vanished.

"He's gone," Scotty said, disappointed. "He must have come to and beat it." He looked at the mixed group of workers and fishermen who had followed him, and he missed a familiar face. "Hey, where's Mike Kozac?"

No one knew. Scotty scratched his head. First Rick, now Mike. Had they gone together?

"They may have seen who threw the grenades," Tom speculated. "Maybe they went after them."

The whine of sirens sounded down the road toward Crayville, and in a moment two cruisers loaded with State Police screamed to a stop before the plant. The officers piled out, and a sergeant demanded, "Who phoned there was a riot starting here?"

"I did." Doug stepped forward. "It's over," he said. "You're a little late."

"We came as fast as we could," the sergeant said curtly.

The doctor arrived from Crayville, and was directed to the wounded man. Not until he was attended and taken away in the doctor's car did they settle down to talk to the police sergeant.

Tom told the story from beginning to end while the sergeant took notes. Then the officer asked questions, piecing out the story. Doug advanced his theory that the fight had been a cover-up for the men who had thrown the bombs.

"Got any proof?" the officer asked. "Or are you just speculating?"

"It's only a theory," Doug admitted, "but it fits the facts."

"I think it's enough to start on. Where can I find this Cunner Stoles?"

"He hangs out at Zukky's Restaurant on the water front," Scotty supplied quickly.

Tom leafed through the phone book. "His address is 15 Whaler Street."

"Okay. Now, I think we'll want a talk with this fore-man of yours."

Tom supplied the address Tony had used.

"What about the poison?" Scotty asked.

"We'll notify the Coast Guard. They'll take samples and have them analyzed. Now, if you want to press charges against these fishermen, you have a right to."

"Forget it," Tom said. "They're plenty sorry for what happened."

"All right. We'll keep you posted if we find anything." The officer rose and went out to the cruisers. The fishermen had gathered in a group by themselves and were watching the troopers nervously.

Doug went over to them.

"It's okay. We're not pressing charges."

There was a mass sigh of relief.

"And you needn't worry any more about this plant," Doug added bitterly. "It's going out of business before it even gets started." He turned and strode back to the Quonset hut.

One more item, Tom had said, and they would be finished. Scotty knew that the tanks were damaged beyond repair, the special chrome alloy finish torn and twisted. He followed the partners into the hut, his shoulders sagging. Too bad for it to end this way.

"I wish I knew where Rick went," he said.

"Probably for help," Tom guessed. "He'll be back before long."

"This washes us up," Doug said. "There's no point in keeping the workmen on. Tom, will you and Scotty take them back to Bridgeport? I'll make an estimate of the damage."

"Okay."

The workmen were waiting outside. Tom addressed them. "I'm sorry, fellows, but that bombing just blasted us out of business. If you'll gather round as I call out your names, we'll pay you for the day's work, with a little extra bonus for loyalty. Then we'll take you back."

Scotty went over to the truck Tony had driven and

climbed into the driver's seat. Rick would be back by the time he returned from Bridgeport. Then they might just as well go home to Spindrift.

"The police won't find out much," he voiced his thoughts aloud. "There's no proof against anyone, not even Cunner."

Presently the men climbed aboard and he headed the truck for Bridgeport, following Tom's truck. It was after four o'clock when the two trucks pulled into the plant yard again.

Doug was sitting on the Quonset hut steps. He called a greeting and gestured toward two large packing boxes. "Company came while you were gone."

Scotty read the labels. They were from the Carstairs Manufacturing Company. "The fractionator units," he said.

"Yes. And a lot of good they'll do now," Tom murmured.

"Did Rick come back?" Scotty asked.

"Not yet. And I haven't heard from him," Doug replied.

"That's funny," Scotty said.

He had been positive that Rick would be waiting at the plant. He sat down and thought it over. The Cub wouldn't still be in the air after so many hours. But where had it landed? Spindrift? He rejected the idea that Rick had gone home.

Maybe Steve Hollis had seen him. Scotty went into

the hut and called the airport. He waited, fidgeting, while Steve came to the phone.

"This is Don Scott," he said. "I was with Rick Brant the other day. Have you seen him?"

"Seen him? And how! He landed here like a visiting hurricane. I didn't have a chance to talk with him. He said he was following someone and needed a car, so I lent him mine. What's it all about, anyway?"

"Search me," Scotty said. "Which way did he go?"

"Last I saw, he was heading for the parkway."

"Thanks," Scotty said, and rang off.

He went back to where the partners were sitting in silent gloom, and he was very thoughtful. Following someone? It had to be one of the bomb throwers, or both, if there had been two. Steve hadn't mentioned Mike Kozac. If someone had been with Rick, he would have mentioned it.

"Rick went after the bomb throwers," he told the partners, and gave them the details of the conversation.

"I hope he doesn't catch up with them!" Tom exclaimed.

"I hope," Scotty echoed. He had to assume that the man or men who had thrown the bombs were the same ones who had sealed them in the fractionator. It offered unpleasant possibilities. If they got their hands on Rick . . . "He wouldn't do anything without me," Scotty said, with more assurance than he felt. "He'll track them to where they're going, then he'll phone.

Wait and see. And where do you suppose Mike Kozac went?"

The partners didn't have even the glimmer of an idea.

Scotty got up and wandered down to the sediment tanks, too upset to keep still. The tanks were a mess. They might be straightened, the shrapnel holes welded, but that wouldn't do much good so far as the chrome finish was concerned.

By five Scotty was so jittery he couldn't stay still for more than a minute.

At six, he had Doug report Rick's disappearance to the State Police.

"They'll send out a description," Doug reported. "They can't do much else for the time being."

By seven o'clock, Scotty was certain that the bomb throwers had Rick, had undoubtedly murdered him, and were disposing of the body. He racked his brains for a clue. Where had Rick gone? Who knew where he had gone?

Cunner Stoles!

On the instant he was legging it toward town. He'd find Cunner if he had to take the town apart, then he'd choke the information out of him. He barged in through the door of Zukky's and found the place deserted. The fishermen evidently had no desire to congregate in their favorite spot after the day's events. The counterman was polishing the counter with what seemed to be the same dirty towel, the same toothpick in his mouth.

"Where's Cunner?"

The counterman glanced up quickly, then dropped his eyes again.

"Ain't seen him."

"Where's Cunner?"

The counterman threw down the towel. "I told you I don't know! Why'nt you ask the cops? They came lookin' for him, too. How do I know? Do I keep track of the bum?"

It didn't ring true. Old Bill Shakespeare had written something about people who protested too much. Scotty leaned across the counter. One tanned fist grabbed the lapels of the dirty jacket and jerked forward. The counterman turned white.

"Where's Cunner?"

"I told you I don't know." The words were a whine.

Scotty's fist tightened the lapels. The man's face turned red and he choked.

"Where's Cunner?"

He cocked a fist back and stared into the counterman's eyes. The eyes shifted, fell. "You won't hit me if I tell?"

"Give, and quick!"

"He got a phone call, maybe five minutes ago. He was hidin' in the back room. He went out like a shot, headin' for his boat. That's all I know, mister."

Scotty was gone on the echo. He sprinted along the boardwalk and turned down the pier, not stopping until he reached the berth where Cunner's boat had been tied.

It was gone!

For a moment he knew dark despair, then he heard the engine, and he saw the low lines of the dragger. It was standing off the plant, heading south!

Scotty didn't bother using the road. He went along the water front, dodging buildings, piles of lobster pots, leaping over smaller obstacles. At last he gained the open beach and ran all out until he came to the plant. There were no keys to the plant motorboat; the ignition was turned on by connecting two wires. He twisted them together and punched the starter. The engine roared into life and he cast off, heading after Cunner.

Not until he was well away from the pier did it occur to him that he should have told the partners. Well, it was too late now; he couldn't take time to go back. He opened the throttle wide and went after the dragger.

The spray in his face and the wind across the bow cooled his temper somewhat and he began to think. After all, Cunner wouldn't know where Rick had gone. But he might know where to locate Tony, or Lewis. That phone call had probably been from one of them. Why else would he be taking his boat out at this time of night, especially when the police were looking for him?

Scotty had a hunch. Rick would call it a subconscious decision based on facts, but to Scotty it was simply a hunch. The hunch said that Cunner's trip might well have something to do with Rick. He throttled down and swung in toward shore. No use of letting Cunner know he was being followed.

By hugging the shore, ducking in and out of coves, using his superior speed to keep cover, he could trail Cunner. And Cunner wouldn't know, if he stayed far enough back to cover up his engine noise.

Scotty settled down for the chase.

CHAPTER XIV

Fred Lewis's Secret

THE subway train roared into the station Rick had just left and ground to a stop. He looked back, and his heart jumped into his throat and stayed there.

Lewis had jumped down to the track after him!

Rick ran. His only thought was to put as much distance as possible between himself and the nemesis that followed. He ran until he felt the thrumming of the tracks again, then he stepped into one of the niches that had been cut into the concrete of the tunnel wall. He saw Lewis duck into a similar niche, then he flattened out as the train roared past, so close he could have touched it. As the last car passed he jumped out on the tracks again and continued his flight.

There must be openings leading to the street somewhere. It was hard running on the ties. Once he glanced back, and saw that he was gaining a little. Another train roared down on him and he leaped between two pillars to the next track.

Ahead of him he saw lights, and realized that he had run almost to the next station, the Times Square platform. Actually, he had run about seven blocks.

If a train came now he could leap to the platform and board it, and Lewis would have to stand in a niche until the train left.

But luck was not with him. He climbed up on the platform and ran toward the crowd gathered a little distance down. Some of them looked at him curiously, but it is a peculiarity of New Yorkers that the unusual causes little disturbance. They are too intent on their own business. No one attempted to interfere with the wild-eyed boy, nor with the man with the peculiar white face who climbed to the platform after him.

Rick reached the momentary safety of the crowd and sized up his situation. He was on the platform between the downtown local and express tracks. There were stairways here and there, but he didn't know where they led. He started running down the platform, pushing through the subway riders who waited. And then an express pulled into the station.

He kept moving as the express disgorged its crowd of passengers and others began getting aboard. He had to make up his mind in a hurry. He chose the train, pushing in through a door just as it slid shut.

He couldn't be sure that Lewis was on the train, but

he couldn't take a chance. He made his way through the packed crowds, working down toward the extreme front car. The train gathered speed, slowed, jerked to a stop.

Pennsylvania Station!

Rick waited until the last passengers left, then pushed his way through those getting aboard. He kept an eye open for Lewis, and thought he saw him.

Yes! Lewis got off the train, too, and was starting for him!

Across the platform, a local pulled in and its doors slid open. The express was still waiting, to give people a chance to change trains.

Rick faced Lewis, waiting. Lewis waited, too, ready to leap either way.

The crowd thinned. The local started to close its doors. Rick jumped for it and caught a door as it started to slide closed. He held it, waiting. Then he pulled it back and jumped onto the platform again. The door slid closed with a sighing sound. The red lights winked out and the train began to move.

Lewis wasn't in sight!

Rick made a wild jump for the express, and an obliging soldier held the door for him. As the express started, the local roared out of the station. He saw Lewis, his face pressed to the car door, and he waved jauntily.

Success! His quick move had left Lewis on the local;

he was safely on the express, next stop Fourteenth Street, while the man with the white face had several stops to make. Rick breathed freely for the first time and an overwhelming weakness made him lean against the car vestibule wall.

At the next stop he left the subway, heading toward the place where he had parked the car. The envelope under his belt crunched as he walked, and burned his curiosity. He went into a doorway, out of the pedestrian traffic, and took it from under his jacket.

It wasn't sealed. He drew out three eight-by-ten photographs, with as many negatives.

The doorway whirled, gyrated, then steadied. Rick stared at the first picture, completely stunned.

He looked at it again, refusing to believe what he saw until a careful examination showed him that it was true. He sank down on the doorstep and muttered, "Well, I'll be doggoned! Manfred Wessel! But it's impossible!"

The dark-faced, thin-lipped man in the picture had once worked for Rick's father, and had shown every sign of becoming an important scientist. Then he had gone away, and had been next heard of in Germany. Rumor said he had aided the Nazis in the development of the robot bombs, but, since proof was lacking, he hadn't been tried as a war criminal.

Then, when Hartson Brant and his associates were constructing the moon rocket, a mysterious man with a hideously scarred face had appeared, and with the aid of a traitor on the Spindrift staff, had tried to sabotage the experiment while working on a rocket of his own in an effort to win the two-million-dollar Stoneridge grant for advancement of the science of electronics.

Rick's thoughts flashed back to the day of the rocket launching. The man with the scarred face had made a last, desperate attempt to destroy the Spindrift rocket, had been captured and his identity revealed. He was the same scientist who had worked for Rick's father and had later aided the Nazis. Manfred Wessel! His face had been scarred beyond recognition in a chemical explosion sometime in the past.

But Wessel had gotten away from his captors, and, eluding Rick and Scotty, had leaped from the cliff behind the laboratory down to the surf and rocks below. His body had never been recovered, but they had been sure he was dead.

They had been wrong. By some miracle, Wessel had lived. The proof was in Rick's hands.

The first picture was of Wessel as he had looked when he worked for Hartson Brant. The second picture showed how he had looked when he tried to destroy the moon rocket, when his burned face had caused the boys to nickname him "Scarface."

And the third picture was of Fred Lewis!

Fred Lewis was Manfred Wessel!

These were the before-and-after pictures of a plastic

surgery operation—an operation that had been a failure, changing Wessel's face, but leaving it colorless, the skin tightly stretched!

All at once everything was clear.

Lewis—or Wessel—had been the one who had tried to kill them. He had two good reasons: First, revenge, because Rick and Scotty had discovered his plot to wreck the moon rocket, thus preventing him from winning two million dollars and later making him a fugitive from justice. Second, he had been afraid they would recognize Fred Lewis as Manfred Wessel!

The second reason accounted for the telegram. He had sent it, hoping to keep them away from Crayville. That was why it had been addressed to "Rick." Wessel had known his nickname!

Rick knew it had to be true, but it was hard to believe. Hadn't he and Scotty seen Wessel leap to his death? But he had survived, to become Fred Lewis, and to continue his life of crime by trying now to wreck the sea mine plant.

He looked at the pictures again, and examined the envelope. Inside he found a slip of paper.

"I.O.U. $3,500 for plastic surgery operation. M.W."

This was the hold the businessman in the restaurant had on Wessel. The police would be after the renegade scientist, once they knew he had survived the jump from the cliff. A stiff prison sentence awaited him for what he had done to wreck the Spindrift rocket.

Now that Rick realized what he had found, he was nervous. It wouldn't do to carry such dynamite around with him. A mailbox caught his eye. He hurried up the street and found a drugstore that had a stamp vending machine, and inserted three dimes. Eighteen cents should be enough. He borrowed a pen from the druggist and then hesitated. Where should he send it? He couldn't put anyone he knew in jeopardy, in case Wessel found out.

He finally addressed it to himself, care of *General Delivery, Milford.* Then he went to the mailbox and dropped it in. Not until the metal door clanged shut did he breathe easily.

Now to get Steve's car and head back to Crayville! He crossed near the garage where Lewis had gone only after a long survey showed him that the man with the white face was not in sight. Steve's car was right where he had left it. He walked up to it, searching in his pocket for the keys, and a voice hailed him.

"Got a match, bud?"

He whirled, and all the color drained from his face. Standing in a doorway, grinning, was Tony Larzo! And Wessel! He started to run, but Tony moved faster. He took Rick's arm and twisted it until he gasped with pain.

"Let's go," Tony said. "In the car, punk." He opened the door and pushed Rick in. "Where are the keys?"

Rick's lips clamped shut. He was sick with realizing how easily he had walked into the trap, but he was puzzled, too. How had they known?

"Search him," Wessel rasped. He slid in behind the wheel.

Tony's hands patted his pockets, found the right one, came up with the key.

"One squawk out of you and you're all done," Tony warned.

The coupé swung away from the curb, circled the block, then turned in at the garage. It was empty, except for the black sedan.

"Out," Tony commanded.

Rick got out; there was nothing else he could do. They marched him into a back room and pushed him into a kitchen chair. Wessel patted his clothes rapidly, then straightened up with a snarl.

"Where's that envelope?"

Rick stared at him dully. An open hand caught him on the side of the face, sending a wave of pain through him.

"Talk!"

Another slap.

"I can't think," he managed. "Honest. I was so surprised . . ."

Wessel permitted himself a grim smile. "We thought you would be. You were so smug when you waved at me . . . I began to think. You must have trailed me by car, although I don't know just how. No one followed me from the plant. And if that were true, you must have parked near by. I left the subway, took a cab directly here. Tony had arrived, and we simply searched until we found a car just around the corner with Connecticut license plates. And now, where is that envelope?"

There was no mercy in the white face. Rick knew he could expect none. Wessel hated him. But as long as the whereabouts of the envelope remained a mystery, he was safe, to some extent. They might torture him, but they wouldn't dare kill him. At least that was his hope. He closed his mouth tight and gritted his teeth.

Another slap rocked him and almost knocked him from the chair. As though through a mist he saw the white face of Wessel, the dark complexion of Tony Larzo.

Slap! Slap! One side, then the other. The air was pink now, and his eyes wouldn't focus.

"We can't stay here," Tony's voice said from far away. "Someone is apt to walk in."

"You're right," Wessel said. "Okay, Tony, give it to him."

Rick sensed the coming blow and tried to duck. The room exploded, then faded into darkness. His limp body sagged from the chair to the floor.

CHAPTER XV

Shadows in the Night

HAD Scotty guessed what had happened to Rick, he would have been frantic. As it was, he was being pushed to the near edge of erupting like a dark-haired volcano. The reason was Cunner's peculiar actions.

Scotty had followed the dragger, keeping at a safe distance, until darkness began to close down. Then he had followed the white light at the stern of Cunner's boat. He couldn't be sure how far they had come: he knew only that they had passed no towns. By the scent in the air, they were close by extensive salt-water marshes.

Cunner alternately throttled down, then speeded up again, but at his fastest, he never exceeded five knots. Scotty figured that he was deliberately killing time, so that he wouldn't get to some mysterious rendezvous too soon.

He glanced at his watch. It was almost nine. He shook

169

it to see if it were running. Surely more time than that had passed!

Up ahead, the lights of Cunner's boat moved lazily. Scotty tried to relax, but there was too much tension in him. If only he could be certain that the water trail would lead to Rick! He had a hunch that Rick desperately needed him. He might even have phoned the plant to call for aid.

Suddenly Scotty straightened, eyes trying to pierce the darkness ahead. Cunner was swinging into shore.

Scotty killed his engine and drifted, listening. He heard the coughing sound of the dragger's exhaust, saw the lights move toward the dark bulk of shore. He thought he could make out some kind of building, but he wasn't sure.

He had been hugging the shore pretty well, now the incoming tide and the swell pushed the motorboat toward the tree-shrouded bank. That was good; he needn't risk starting the engine again.

In a short while the craft grounded gently and he leaped ashore, carrying a rope. He snubbed it around a tree root that jutted toward the water and secured it. Then he began to make his way through the dark underbrush toward the place where Cunner had pulled in.

Scotty was at home in the woods, even in the darkness. He moved swiftly, silently, and presently came to the edge of a clearing. There was a building there, an abandoned barn, from the look of it. A small pier jutted

into the water, and Cunner was tying up to it. After a
moment he switched off the dragger's lights, and there
was only the glow of a pipe.

The waiting was hard. Scotty chafed with impatience,
but he didn't move. He lay at full length, screened by
underbrush. Mosquitoes settled on his exposed ankles
and had a banquet. He made no move toward them. He
was taking no chances of giving away his presence.

After what couldn't have been more than five minutes
but seemed like eternity, he heard a car engine. In a
moment head lamps cut a swath through the woods
and the car rolled into the clearing, pulled up to the
dock, and stopped. The engine died and the lights went
off.

Scotty could see only dimly. Objects appeared to be
shadows rather than substance. He heard the car doors
open, heard subdued voices. Two men got out of the
car, reached in, dragged something out. A third person!
Scotty saw them half carry, half drag the limp figure
toward Cunner's boat.

Fear took his heart and twisted it.

Who was it that they carried?

CHAPTER XVI

Swim—or Die!

RICK was smothering, the weight of a ton of wool pushing him down. A sudden bump jolted his teeth together. He struggled to rise, and a harsh voice warned him:

"Stay put or you'll get slugged again."

A foot pushed at him. The voice and the foot belonged to Tony Larzo.

Things began to make some kind of sense. He was on the floor of a car. He could feel the harsh floor rug and the footrest. Yes, he was in the back seat, and there was a blanket over him. He pushed the blanket aside and cool air swept into his parched lungs.

His head ached unbearably. He put up an exploring hand and found a lump the size of an egg. No, two lumps. One above his forehead, the other behind his ear. He looked up at the window and saw that it was dark.

The bumping continued rhythmically, each stroke curling in his tortured head like a whiplash. After a while he identified it. Those were the tar expansion joints in a concrete highway.

Tony spoke from above him. "He's coming to. Shall I sap him again?"

Manfred Wessel's hated voice answered from the front seat. "No need. We'll be turning off the parkway in a minute. Let him yell if he wants to. No one will hear."

They were on the Merritt Parkway then, and about to turn off it. Much time had passed that he couldn't account for. He had a dim recollection of trying to sit up, and then something hit him. He pieced together the broken bits of memory and they added up all right.

Tony had knocked him out, back at the garage. Then they had put him in the sedan, perhaps immediately, perhaps not until later, because that must have been almost four hours ago. And after a while they had headed for Connecticut. He probably had come to life sometime during the trip, and Tony had slugged him again.

Rick's analysis was all right, so far as it went. What he could not know was that Wessel had tried to force a dose of chloral hydrate knockout drops into him at the garage. He had swallowed some, but not enough to keep him drugged for the entire trip. He had shown signs of returning consciousness at a gasoline station, while Wessel was telephoning Cunner, and Tony had hit him again.

He lay quietly, gathering his strength. A break might come, and he wanted to be ready for it. The sedan turned sharply, piling him in a corner. Tony cursed and kicked at him. The bumping of the expansion joints gave way to the smooth hum of tarvia or macadam surfacing. Rick let his mind float off into misty darkness and let his body relax. His time wasn't here yet. He needed all the strength he could muster.

After a while the sedan made another sharp turn, and the joggling ride told Rick they were on a back road, probably dirt. It seemed to grow worse. His chance might come on this road, if they slowed enough. Little by little he began to gather his legs under him.

The sedan slowed. Rick looked up, past Tony's head, and saw the dark outlines of trees silhouetted against the lighter darkness of the sky. The sedan slowed even more and crept over some obstacle in the road.

Rick tensed. Now! Now, before they gathered speed again. Soundlessly, with all the drive in his legs, he threw himself upward and forward, reaching for the door handle. He gained it! The door swung open!

Something descended with stunning force on his head and the strength flowed out of him. Hands reached out and dragged him back. He fought to keep from losing consciousness, and partially succeeded, but his body refused to obey. He was paralyzed, temporarily unable to move as much as a finger.

Dimly, he heard the car door slam, and voices talking. He didn't know what they said; he didn't care.

The sedan moved ahead, and presently it swung in a half circle and stopped. Tony got out, stumbling over him. Wessel got out, too.

They reached in and dragged him out, and carried him across rattling boards, his legs dragging. They carried him in through an open door into light that blinded him, and they put him in a chair. He sat upright, his head lolling, and he felt ropes being passed around his arms, around his legs.

Cold water smashed into his face. He shuddered, and the haze cleared. After a moment he looked up, into three faces. When had Cunner come? He couldn't remember.

"Well, Brant?" Wessel said harshly.

Rick looked up at Wessel and tried to make his face expressionless.

"There's no one within miles of here. You can yell as much as you like. And you will, too, before we're through. Unless you make things easy on yourself and tell me what you did with that envelope."

Rick set his jaw stubbornly and met the renegade scientist's eyes unflinchingly. Even when Tony slapped him he didn't take his eyes away.

Cunner winced. "Stop that!"

"Shut up. Listen, I know how to make this bird talk," Tony grated.

"Go ahead," Wessel said.

Tony reached into his pocket and came out with a jackknife. He pressed a spring and a gleaming blade snapped open. Rick saw the cabin light reflected from it and a deep shudder racked him.

"Talk," Tony said, "or I'll cut my initials on your face!"

The blade was a magnet, drawing his eyes. He saw a tiny nick on the point, almost microscopic in size. He swallowed hard. The blade came closer, was only inches from his face.

The blade touched his forehead, pressed . . .

A form hurtled through the door and grabbed Tony's arm. Incredulously Rick saw Scotty! He saw him lift and twist, heard Tony's scream, saw the knife go flying and heard the sickening crack of Tony's arm.

Wessel leaped on Scotty's back, and miraculously continued right over the boy's head, to land with a stunning crash against a bulkhead.

Rick saw Cunner step in and opened his mouth to shout a warning, but he was too late. Cunner swung, a huge lead sinker held in his hand. Scotty sank to the deck.

In brief seconds hope had flared and died. Now Scotty would have to take Wessel's vengeance, too.

Hopelessly, Rick saw Tony rise and launch a vicious

kick at the unconscious boy's ribs. The dark foreman was clutching a wrist that dangled at an odd angle.

Wessel got to his feet, his eyes venomous. Cunner looked ready to cry.

"Where did he come from?" Wessel demanded. "He must have followed you, you fool!" His open hand rocked Cunner's head back. "Tie him up."

Cunner obeyed like a man in a dream. In a moment Scotty was tightly trussed. Already he was stirring, and a groan escaped his lips.

"He must have a boat near by," Wessel said. "Scatter and find it. All of us. If he followed you, perhaps others did, too. We've got to get out of here."

They hurried out to the dock, leaving the boys alone.

"Scotty," Rick called. "Scotty!"

"Huh?"

Scotty managed to sit up, resting against the bulkhead, his hands tied behind him.

"My head! Who hit me?"

"Cunner. Scotty, you shouldn't have come!"

"Yes, I should. Only I should have brought a shotgun. Rick, tell them what they want to know. What is it, anyway?"

Rick explained rapidly about the envelope and Scotty whistled, his eyes wide.

"Wessel!"

Rick saw realization dawn in his friend's face. Wessel . . . they didn't have a chance.

"What did you do with it?" Scotty asked quietly.

"I mailed it. To myself." Rick heard a faint scrape from outside the cabin door and knew someone was listening. "At General Delivery, Bridgeport," he finished quickly.

"Thank you. I rather thought you would confide in your friend," Wessel said from the doorway. "Now that we know, the rest is simple. Tony will become Mr. Rick Brant, for purposes of retrieving that envelope. I will see that he is provided with suitable identification."

He went through Rick's pockets rapidly and came up with his wallet. "Something in here will do nicely, I'm sure."

Scotty spoke from the floor. "That plastic surgeon didn't do such a hot job, did he? He changed you from a gargoyle into a monster."

Wessel's eyes flamed, but he merely chuckled. "And you, my young friend, will soon be changed into fish bait."

Tony and Cunner appeared.

"The boat's around the point," Tony said. "We can pick it up. Now, how about fixing this arm?"

Cunner applied a rude splint, then went out to cast off. He kicked the engine into action and the boat shuddered. Rick's glance was anguished as he looked at Scotty.

Fish bait!

The dragger circled around and there was a pause

while Cunner went out and secured the motorboat to the stern with a length of line. Then he pointed the nose straight out into the Sound.

"We have quite a ride," Wessel said conversationally. "Are you familiar with Long Island Sound at this particular place? No? Then let me inform you. It is about sixteen miles wide. We must find the exact middle. Can you imagine why?"

There were fine beads of sweat on Scotty's face. Rick's throat had dried up and he could feel the pulse in his temples.

"I know you are good swimmers," Wessel said. "But are you good enough to swim eight miles? I think not."

"No," Cunner whispered. "We can't do that!"

"And why not, my fat friend?"

"It's murder!"

Tony lunged forward. "Yeah. And you're in it, Cunner, up to your fat neck. If we hang for it, you hang right alongside of us. This will shut your mouth, you weak sister! You won't dare to talk now."

Cunner lapsed into silence, his mouth working.

Sprindrift, Rick thought. We'll never see . . . he started talking, intent on keeping his mind from what was ahead.

"What do you get out of this, Wessel? What's that job your friend is going to give you?"

"Ah, you overheard, eh? Well, that gentleman is going to own the sea mine processes within a week. He'll operate them on a scale your two foolish employers never dreamed of! And I will head the research laboratories. I will come into my own, as I would have once before if you two had not interfered." He laughed. "You won't interfere again."

"You're supposed to be dead," Scotty said.

"Yes. And very convenient, too. To satisfy your curiosity, I will explain. When I jumped from the cliff, it was not for suicidal purposes. There was considerable risk, I admit. But I am a powerful swimmer. You were so sure I had perished that your search was not very thorough. I hid behind a boulder, and when it was dark I made my way to the mainland. The gentleman Brant saw with me came to my assistance. I had known him before. In fact, I did some work for him along the line of cartels while I was in Europe. He arranged for a plastic surgeon to make me over. Not a good job, I fear, but sufficient to hide my identity."

"You were afraid we would recognize you. That's why you locked us in the fractionator," Rick guessed. "With Tony's help."

"Precisely. Of course, I had an added incentive. I derived a great deal of pleasure from imagining your terrors when you found you could not get out. I was quite disappointed."

He stopped smiling suddenly. "But enough of this. I'm sure you will enjoy the ride more if we give you an opportunity to meditate on your past sins. There will be no future ones, I assure you. I cannot afford to let you tell people that I am alive." He turned abruptly and went on deck. Tony followed him.

Cunner was holding the wheel, staring straight ahead.

"Listen," Rick whispered. "You don't want to get mixed up in this, Cunner."

"I don't want to," Cunner mumbled, "but I got to. They'd kill me. You see how they are."

Tony thrust his head through the door. "No more talk, or *three* of you will be shark bait. Got it, Cunner?"

Silence settled in the cabin, except for the throb of the engine. Rick tested his bonds and found them tight. He saw Scotty squirm, and then relax, and knew his friend was tightly tied, too.

His vivid imagination raced ahead. He bit his lip and tried not to think. The pounding of the engine jarred at his thoughts. Each turn of the screw, each beat of the exhaust . . . their remaining time was measured by the engine. He closed his eyes. Not a chance . . . not a single chance. If only Scotty hadn't come!

The dragger lifted to the swells and the engine beat out its rhythmic tempo. Water underneath. And eight miles to shore. How far straight down?

The steady pound of the exhaust measured the miles and the minutes. Rick opened his eyes and saw Scotty watching him. Scotty grinned, and a lump came up in Rick's throat. It wasn't much of a grin. It was strained and it was feeble, but it was nevertheless a grin. He returned it, and his face felt stiff when he smiled. Then the beat of the engine intruded again, hammering against his mind, forcing him to think ahead. Eight miles . . . eight terrible miles . . . and he was weak from the beating he had taken.

"*Eight*," the exhaust said. "*Eight-eight-eight-eight-eight-eight* . . ."

Wessel's voice was loud. "All right, Cunner, shut it off."

The engine beat died, and the silence was even worse.

Tony produced a gun with his good hand. "I'd like an excuse," he said. "In the stomach. It hurts, in the stomach."

"Don't try to fight," Scotty said sharply, and Rick stared. Not fight? Go out without a struggle? It would be better to get shot. Scotty saw his expression and said firmly, "No fight!"

He nodded. Cunner cut his bonds and helped him to his feet. Rick swayed unsteadily.

Cunner lifted Scotty to his feet and cut him loose. Tony's gun wavered between them with dreadful impartiality.

"Out on deck," Wessel ordered.

Rick stumbled on the step and almost fell. He got out on deck and leaned against the cabin wall. Scotty followed him.

"Better hitch a few hunks of scrap iron to 'em," Tony said harshly.

"No, that wouldn't do. The draggers and trawlers have a way of cleaning the bottom too thoroughly. They might be found too soon," Wessel objected.

"Well, I can at least knock 'em in the head," Tony growled.

"No, Tony. If they are washed ashore, we want the autopsy to show death by drowning."

It was a dream, a nightmare. Even official hangmen never talked in this calm tone of voice. He would wake up. When he hit the water he would wake up, and he would find himself safe in bed at Spindrift. He clung to the thought.

"Open the sea cocks in their boat, Cunner."

Cunner moved to obey. There was gurgling from the motorboat. Cunner untied it. In an incredibly short time it filled. Then there were only bubbles.

"Who is first?" Wessel asked. "Scotty? Marines volunteer for anything."

"Sure," Scotty said amiably.

"In a moment," Rick thought, "I'll wake up. When I hit the water I'll wake up."

Scotty disappeared in a froth of bubbles.

Rick walked like a sleepwalker to the side of the dragger. Now! He'd wake up now. Cold water engulfed him, filled his mouth, his nose. He sank, and the chill of the water penetrated and his head cleared and he knew he wasn't dreaming.

A hand grabbed his collar and pulled him up.

"Swim," Scotty commanded. "Tread water!"

"Yes," a voice said from above them. It mingled with the sudden bark of the engine. "Yes, my young friends! Swim—or die!"

CHAPTER XVII

An Angel in a Lobster Smack

THE dragger gathered speed, its bow lifting. Rick watched it go, hungrily, hopelessly. He was treading water automatically, his eyes fixed on the stern light. It dwindled, became a distant star, winked out. They were alone now—eight miles from shore.

Scotty's voice cut into his despair. "Okay! Get out of your pants and drop your shoes."

"What?"

"Come on! We're not giving up yet. Why do you think I told you not to struggle on the boat? We have an ace up our sleeves, old son. But we needed all our strength. Now, get out of those pants, and quick!"

He couldn't guess what Scotty meant, but he knew that tone of voice. He lifted his legs, letting himself sink as he fumbled with his shoelaces. The knots came undone with a little tugging and the shoes drifted silently downward. Then Rick unbuckled his belt and

slipped out of his trousers, holding to them and await-
ing further instructions.

"Now tie a knot in each leg."

It was hard work, managing the wet cloth, but he
succeeded.

"Now watch me."

Scotty held his own trousers by the tops and whipped
them through the air over his head. They caught the
air, ballooned out slightly. Then he thrust the top down
under the water. The air-filled legs thrust up like two
oversize sausages.

Rick got the idea immediately. He tried it, and after
a moment got the knack of inflating the wet trousers.
Then, holding the open top downward with both hands,
he rested between the inflated legs. They acted just
like water wings!

"The cloth is too porous to hold air for long," Scotty
said. "We'll have to keep doing it. They taught it to us
in the service. I knew a sailor once who kept afloat this
way for thirty hours before he was picked up."

"But . . ."

"No buts! We'll make it. Just keep moving a little so
your arms and legs won't get numb. And no more talking. We'll need our breath. This is going to be hard
work."

Some of Scotty's hopefulness caught him. They
weren't done yet!

Scotty paddled close. From his shirt pocket he took
a small scrap of paper.

"Watch this." He cast it adrift. It sank almost at once, but not before they saw it drifting away from them. "The current is toward Long Island. It's about high tide now, and the tide will be running out soon, too. All we have to do is stay afloat and we'll end up on Long Island."

They fell silent. The faintly luminous swells lifted them, dropped them. Now and then one of them whipped his trousers through the air to refill them. The water brought a kind of spreading numbness, so that after a while Rick wasn't even conscious of his body. To inflate the trousers was automatic. His mind seemed insulated from the sea and the darkness. He didn't even notice the crescent moon that floated up out of the farther dark.

"Rick! Rick!"

He came out of the half-daze into which his mind had drifted. "What?"

"Are you all right?"

"Yes. You?"

"Okay. I didn't see you moving."

How much time had passed? How far had they floated? He was tiring fast. It was a painful effort now to lift the trousers above water to inflate them. He couldn't last much longer. A time would come when his aching arms would refuse to lift, and the last air would seep from the tied trouser legs, and he would struggle just a little before sinking.

How far is down? It really didn't matter. Six feet or

six hundred, it was all the same. The numbness flowed over him again and he pinched his arm, hard. There was only a faint response of pain. He tried to slap himself in the face, but only dashed water into his eyes.

A sodden mass floated by him, and in the dim light he saw a white face. Strange . . . very strange . . . was someone else around? A faint message from his memory stirred his senses. Suddenly he yelled:

"Scotty! Wake up, Scotty!" He found the power to kick, to push himself toward the other boy.

"Hmm? Wha' say?"

"Scotty!"

He reached him, slapped him hard. His palm didn't even tingle, but Scotty shook his head and straightened up.

"Thanks," he said simply. "Thanks, Rick."

Scotty was the stronger of the two, and Scotty was so tired that he had drifted off. Utter hopelessness gripped Rick. No chance, no chance at all. Why prolong the agony? It would be so easy to let go. They would drift downward, moving gently in the current, and they would sleep, deeply, without dreams.

He struggled with the temptation to let go of his trousers, and he won. He kicked feebly and reinflated the trousers. Wessel hadn't won yet!

How long had it been? He made himself think. Time is important. But time is relative. During vacation, days turned into hours, weeks into days, months into weeks.

There weren't really three months in a vacation, but only three weeks, because you enjoyed yourself. But here, in the dark sea, a second became a minute. A minute was an hour. And an hour was eternity. They had been floating for about ten eternities.

The minutes that seemed to be hours blended and were one with the unceasing lapping of the water. He tried watching the moon; he had just discovered it. Moonrise wasn't until almost one o'clock, was it? Had so much time passed? When he watched, it floated in the sea of darkness and didn't advance. But when he looked away and made himself think, and then looked back, it had sneaked upward, toward the zenith. It became a game. He tried to outwit the moon, to look away, then look up before it had a chance to move. It was angry, because he was winning. He knew the moon was angry, because it had turned pale. He laughed, and chose the wrong moment to laugh. He gulped salt water and choked. The choking brought him back to full consciousness and he called:

"Scotty! Scotty!"

"I'm okay, Rick. What is it?"

"Dawn! It's almost daylight!" That was why the moon had grown pale.

"Who's there?"

"It's me, you dope! What's the matter, Scotty?"

Scotty's voice sounded strange. "I didn't say anything."

The sense of that penetrated, and then they were both yelling. A voice hailed them and an angel appeared, an angel in a tattered sweater and disreputable hat, and his chariot was a lobster smack.

The angel extended a golden wand—or perhaps it was only a boat hook.

"Grab aholt," he said, in a very prosaic voice. "We'll have ye out o' there in two shakes."

CHAPTER XVIII

Setting the Trap

"THAT's about all there is to it," Rick said. "The lobster-man—his name was Jake Bray—took us to his house. Mrs. Bray made us eat breakfast, then I called you. Then she insisted that we go to bed, and we slept from about six until eight this evening."

"Mr. Bray went out and bought sneakers for us," Scotty added, "because we'd dropped our shoes in the water. Then, when we woke up, he drove us into Port Jefferson. We caught the ferry to Bridgeport and took a bus, and here we are."

Tom Blakely and Doug Chambers looked at each other and shook their heads, then they looked at the boys again.

"If you'd lend me a few choice hairs off that rabbit's-foot you carry, I'd appreciate it," Tom said.

"I could use a couple, too," Doug added grimly. "I've never heard of such phenomenal luck."

"We were lucky, all right," Rick admitted. "But Scotty's knowing how to make water wings of our pants helped plenty, too. Now suppose you bring us up to date."

"Well, Tom called the police right after you phoned," Doug said. "They sent out an alarm for Wessel, Tony, and Cunner, but they've had no success thus far. They promised to let us know."

"I'll feel better when Wessel is safely in the clink," Scotty remarked. "We've had trouble enough from that bird. I hope he gets a hundred years at hard labor."

"How old a man is Wessel?" Tom asked.

"I don't know exactly," Rick said. "Not very old, anyway. Maybe forty. And he's in good shape, believe me. The way he kept up with me in New York scared me silly."

"Remember how he got away from us and jumped off the cliff at Spindrift?" Scotty reminded him. "He's a pretty good athlete."

There was an interruption as one of the guards knocked at the door. The guards were ex-policemen who looked capable of dealing with anything that came up. They were armed, and on their toes.

"A guy out here wants to come in," the guard said. "Says his name is Curtis."

"We've been expecting him," Doug said. "Let him in."

Rick looked toward the door curiously. Curtis? The name wasn't familiar.

The door opened and Mike Kozac came in!

"Mike!" Scotty jumped to his feet. "Where did you go?"

Rick had heard of Mike's disappearance. He chimed in, "Yes, and since when is your name Curtis?"

Mike grinned. "All my life. Once a Curtis, always a Curtis."

The boys stared. Mike's accent had vanished. He looked different, too, in a well-tailored tweed suit and a soft hat.

Tom took the floor, grinning widely. "You two aren't the only ones with surprises. Boys, meet Mr. Michael Curtis, head of Curtis Investigations."

"Best detective agency in New York," Mike added with a smile.

"Well, I'm beat!" Scotty exclaimed, and Rick echoed him.

"Mike phoned this morning," Doug explained. "He was hired by my Uncle Frank to investigate the trouble we've been having, and, unknown to us, he's been on the job for two weeks."

Mike took a chair and straddled it. "That's right. I've told Doug and Tom some of the story, but I suppose I'd better start at the beginning."

"Yes," Rick agreed. "We want to know all of it."

"Okay," Mike said. "Well, it starts when Mr. Chambers hired me. Doug thought his uncle had invested only ten thousand in the plant because he was stingy, I guess, but that wasn't the reason. Mr. Chambers just didn't want to make things too easy. He believes that young men should work for what they get. Anyway, when he heard of the trouble they'd had, he got worried and hired me to check up. I started by coming to Crayville, as Mike Kozac."

Mike had discovered at once that Cunner was stirring up the fishermen, and had kept an eye on the fat man until he made contact with Fred Lewis—or Wessel. Then the detective had dropped Cunner and trailed the white-faced man for a full week, hoping that Wessel would lead him to the big boss. Mike had discovered that Wessel always parked his car at the same garage, on Eighth Avenue, but the trail had never led to anyone higher up. Instead, it had led back to Crayville, and to Tony Larzo!

The detective had debated telling the partners that Tony was mixed up in a plot against them, and decided against it, on the grounds that it was easier to keep track of a known accomplice. Had they fired Tony, the plotters would have been warned that they were under suspicion and would have covered their tracks better.

On a Sunday, Mike had gone to Zukky's to try to find out how far Cunner's agitation among the fishermen had progressed. The boys had seen him there.

What Mike had learned worried him, and he decided to get a job at the sea mine plant in order to keep a closer watch on Tony, and to be on hand if the fishermen started anything. The recruiting of workmen at Bridgeport had given him his chance. One of his operators had told him about the employment agency that wanted men for the plant; the same operator had driven Mike's car into Crayville on the morning the detective showed up as a workman, and had left it parked in an alley on the edge of town.

The rest was known to the partners and the boys, up to the time of the explosions. Mike, like Rick, had seen the two men in the field. He had seen Wessel leave in his car and Rick run for the Cub. And, like Rick, Mike had chosen to follow Wessel.

"I ran and got my car," he continued. "I saw the Cub go by. I knew Rick was chasing Wessel, but I didn't think he could stay with him. I was sure he was heading for New York, maybe to report to his boss. Instead of trying to chase Wessel down the parkway, and perhaps have him find out he was being followed, I cut across the truck road to Bridgeport, breaking every speed law ever invented. I knew there was a train at 12:33 that would beat Wessel into New York. Well, I made it, but only by luck. It was five minutes late. I got to New York, took a taxi to the garage—where I figured Wessel was heading—and waited on the corner. Sure enough, he showed up. And who should come pussyfooting behind him, but our friend Brant!"

"But I didn't see you!" Rick exclaimed.

Mike grinned. "You weren't supposed to. Because, if he found out you were trailing him and shook you off, I'd still be with him. But you stayed with him. Nice going, too. You can have a job any time you want it."

Mike had followed Rick and Wessel to the restaurant, but had remained outside. He saw Wessel go into the booth with his friend, and saw Rick follow. In a few moments Rick came running out, with Wessel behind him.

"I thought you'd shake him with no trouble," Mike explained, "or I would have given you a hand. But I figured seeing him with his friend was a big break, so I let you and Wessel go, and I followed his pal."

Rick couldn't sit still. "He's the big boss, Mike! Who is he? Where did he go?"

"Easy." Mike grinned. "You'll get high blood pressure. He led me to an office in the RCA building. I got chummy with his receptionist and got some good leads. I spent today tracking them down, and now I have the full story."

All of them were leaning forward now, their full attention on Mike.

"Our friend," he continued, "is Mr. J. Arthur Brink, president of Amalgamated Mines, Inc. And today I found out that he is also the principal stockholder of the Carstairs Company!"

The pieces of the puzzle clicked into place.

Brink had learned about Doug's processes when the young engineer first approached Amalgamated! Then, when the partners refused to sell out, Brink had gone after them in his own way. He had used Wessel, Tony, and Cunner to slow down the plant construction and to sabotage the work. Meanwhile, he had given orders to Carstairs, the plant's biggest creditor. Now, with the bombing of the tanks as the final straw, Carstairs could simply demand payment of their note, and since the partners couldn't meet payment, the plant would be forced into bankruptcy. Then, Carstairs, as their principal creditor, could simply pay off the other creditors and take over the plant and the processes! It was so simple, yet so foolproof that Rick was staggered.

"Then he'll get the plant!" he groaned. "And we can't do anything about it!"

"No," Mike denied. "He won't get the plant. Mr. Chambers has offered to help with enough money to cover the Carstairs note."

Rick and Scotty were about to let out exultant yells, but Mike's next words stopped them.

"He doesn't get the plant, but we don't get him, either. All his business deals have been legitimate, and we'll never prove that he was tied in with Wessel and the others. Seeing him with Wessel means nothing. Wessel and Tony won't talk, and Cunner wouldn't dare. He knows what happens to squealers, even in jail."

The boys and the partners fell silent as the truth of Mike's words became evident. They didn't have a thing on Brink.

Rick remembered the confident, smug face of the businessman as he had teased Wessel about the envelope. He remembered how Brink had smiled as he opened the envelope and glanced through the pictures . . .

"Fingerprints!" he exploded. "Fingerprints on the pictures! Listen, we *have* got him! His fingerprints must be all over those pictures of Wessel!"

"Golly, yes!" Scotty shouted. "That'll prove he knew who Wessel was, and it's a crime to aid a fugitive from justice! And not only that, we can get the others! They'll try to pick up the envelope at Bridgeport! They've probably tried already, but figured the mail was slow."

Mike Curtis looked dazed. "What envelope?" he asked. "What's all this?"

The boys had forgotten that he didn't know Rick's full story. When they had explained, the detective jumped up.

"You're right! We've got all of them cold! Listen, we'll report this to the police. First thing in the morning we'll pick up that envelope at Milford, where Rick actually mailed it, and we'll take a fingerprint expert with us. Brink did some work for the government at one time, so the FBI will have his fingerprints on file! Then we'll go to Bridgeport and help the police set a trap for Wessel and the others. Wessel wouldn't dare *not* to try to get that envelope, and he thinks you two are dead!"

"Won't he be surprised!" Rick exclaimed exultantly.

"Surprised," Scotty chuckled, slapping Rick on the back, "but, brother, he won't be pleased!"

CHAPTER XIX

The Trap Closes

Rick was fidgety. He shifted from one foot to the other and wondered how much longer they would have to wait. He wondered, too, at Scotty's patience. His friend was leaning calmly against a pillar, reading post-office literature.

The boys were in a dim corner of the post office, close to a side door. They had a good view of the front door, through which Wessel and Tony, and perhaps Cunner, would probably come.

Near the front door, Mike Curtis chatted with a husky plain-clothes man of the Bridgeport police force. Mike was dressed in a business suit, and he had a felt hat pulled low over his forehead. Anyone would have to look twice to see any resemblance to the workman, Mike Kozac.

At the other side door, two more plain-clothes officers

waited, with instructions to bar the door if Mike signaled that the fugitives were inside.

Rick glanced at his watch. It was nearing ten o'clock, and they had been waiting since the general delivery window opened at eight. In the preceding hour, they had gone to Milford, accompanied by two State Police officers. The postmaster had opened up early, at their request, and delivered the envelope. The police officers had taken it, unopened. By now they must have classified all the fingerprints on it and teletyped their descriptions to Washington.

"Take it easy, boy," Scotty said. "You're as nervous as a bee in a bird cage."

"I wish something would happen," Rick complained. "I'm getting hungry."

A man next to them said, "You get used to it. Here, have an apple. I always bring a couple along."

Rick stared. Another detective! "How many of you are there?" he asked.

"Eight. We're taking no chances. The outside of the building is covered, too."

Rick wondered where Tom and Doug had gone, and decided they probably had been posted outside, to help the outside police identify the wanted men. He yawned and leaned against a post.

Scotty dug an elbow into his ribs. He looked up, a little irritably.

"Those are my ribs you're breaking, friend."

Then the irritation died, because Scotty was looking at two men who had just come through the side door. The sunlight through the window was in Rick's eyes, so he ducked back for a better look. His breath stopped.

The men were Wessel and Tony Larzo!

He raised his arm, in the agreed-upon signal to Mike, and at that moment Tony glanced around and looked straight into his eyes!

For a shocked instant Tony stared, then he grabbed Wessel and shouted:

"Scram!"

The detective next to the boys leaped forward with a shout, but Tony's foot lifted in a vicious arc and caught the officer in the stomach. Then the two fugitives turned and ran for the side door.

"Get 'em," Scotty shouted, and the two boys sprinted after them.

The officers outside had to be warned! Rick raised his voice in a yell of warning, and bolted through the swinging doors. He caught a glimpse of men running toward him down the sidewalk, then he let out another yell. Cunner Stoles was waiting at the curb in a car, and Wessel and Tony were just opening the door!

Rick made a wild leap, but Scotty was there before him. Tony whirled, a blackjack uplifted. Scotty caught his wrist and twisted. Rick danced around, looking for an opening. Wessel was pushed against the door by Tony and Scotty, and he was struggling to get free.

Tony's other arm lifted, and Rick saw that it was in a plaster cast. The cast descended on Scotty's head.

Scotty fell back for a moment, then his foot shot out and kicked Tony's legs from under him. Wessel, freed, started around the front of the car, but Rick was after him. He charged headlong, and his shoulder caught the fleeing criminal right behind the knees.

It would have brought a penalty for "clipping" on a football field, but here it brought quick victory. Wessel slammed to the cement sidewalk, face first. He didn't even have time to break his fall.

Then, as ready hands lifted Rick to his feet, a police cruiser shot across in front of the getaway car, effectively blocking Cunner's retreat. Tony, who was sprawled against the car, was being dragged to his feet by two officers. Scotty was nursing his knuckles.

Mike Curtis arrived, and Rick saw Tom and Doug sprinting down the sidewalk from the other side of the post office.

"Great going," Mike said. "All three of them at once! Anyone hurt?"

"I saw the dark guy clip Joe with his foot," an officer said, "but he just knocked him down. Everyone else is all right, I guess."

Rick walked over as a husky detective pulled Cunner out of the car by the coat collar.

"Well," Rick said, "if it isn't our fat friend. Surprised to see us, Cunner?"

He was surprised by the man's reaction. Cunner straightened up and met his glance levelly. "You'll never believe this," Cunner said, "but I'm glad it's over. And I'm glad you boys didn't drown. I was afraid I'd never get a good night's sleep again."

Scotty joined Rick. "This life of crime is sure hard on our friend Wessel's face." He grinned. "When you clipped him, he landed nose first. He'll need another plastic surgery job."

"How about Tony?" Rick returned with a smile.

"They'll have to feed him with a spoon," Mike Curtis said from behind them. "Scotty plays rough."

"It was his own fault. He tried to jerk away while I had him in a Japanese wristlock."

"No matter whose fault it is," Mike returned, "he now has two broken wrists. So I guess you boys are even."

A siren put an end to the conversation. The boys watched as the three prisoners were herded into the police wagon. The last thing Rick saw as it drove away was Manfred Wessel. The ex-scientist was holding a blood-soaked handkerchief to his crushed nose, and from above it two dark, venomous eyes glared at the boys.

Later, as the boys and the partners rode back to Crayville in Mike's car, the detective asked them to repeat their story, being careful not to leave anything out, even scraps of conversation.

As they drew up to the plant gate, Mike nodded. "Sorry to make you go all over it again, but I wondered if there might not be something we've overlooked. Are you sure of Wessel's words about his dealings with Brink?"

" 'I did some work for him along the line of cartels in Europe,' " Rick repeated. "I'm sure that was exactly what he said."

"That's how I remember it, too," Scotty said.

"Good. It isn't much, but at least we can ask the Department of Justice to start an investigation into Brink's foreign tie-ups. We may get him on something big yet."

Tom spoke up from the back seat. "When do we find out about the fingerprints?"

"Sometime today, I hope," Mike said.

It was three that afternoon when the phone rang. The State Police wanted to talk with Mike. The private detective took the phone and listened while the officer reported. When he hung up, he was grinning.

"There were three sets of prints," he reported. "Two were identified as Rick's and Wessel's. They had Rick's from his license application, and they had Wessel's from a passport application."

"The third set," Rick prompted. "Come on, Mike!"

"The third set belonged to Mr. Jeremy Arthur Brink. They were nice clear prints. And now the police want to ask Mr. Brink some pointed questions about harboring a known criminal!"

CHAPTER XX

Success!

THE door of the process vault stood open, revealing great banks of electronic tubes. Some of them glowed like radio tubes, but some were a bright, pulsating blue, like mercury vapor lamps. There was a hum, as of a million bees.

Hartson Brant was inspecting everything with scientific interest, but Mrs. Brant and Barby were more interested in the play of iridescent color over the tube banks.

Mike Curtis, Steve Hollis, whose car had been returned by the police, Cap'n Galt, and Uncle Frank Chambers, a distinguished-looking man whom Doug resembled, were standing at the door, chatting. They were interested, of course, but anything as complex as the electronic processes were far afield from their professions and interests.

Rick and Scotty were at the far end of the vault,

watching a series of six heavy glass tanks which looked like the aquarium tanks that goldfish fanciers sometimes use. The tanks were filling slowly with dark, greenish liquid that seemed as thick as syrup.

"Doesn't look much like sea water," Scotty commented.

"It isn't any more," Rick said.

After the sea water passed through the fractionators, the pressure domes, and the sediment tanks, only this stuff, like green molasses, was left.

Clipped to the side of each tank, and projecting down into the liquid, were pairs of gleaming metal rods, called electrodes. Insulated wires led from them to the banks of electronic tubes.

Doug and Tom entered and came to where the boys were watching.

"All okay," Doug said. "Now, let's see what we get."

"It better be something," Tom added, grinning. "With all this audience."

"It will be," Rick said confidently. "You weren't here when we ran the first tests. You'll see."

"No," Tom returned. "While you were playing with all this lovely equipment, I was working hard arranging for buyers for our products. That's what I call real work."

"It's the kind of work I'd like to get." Scotty grinned. "While you were eating at the best hotels and seeing the sights of New York and Philadelphia, we were up to our ears digging ditches, connecting pipes, building platforms, and sweating over hot soldering irons. I'll trade any time."

Doug joined Hartson Brant at the big control panel, and Rick followed, leaving Tom and Scotty exchanging friendly insults by the tanks.

"This is where the equations come in," Doug said. He produced a notebook full of typed computations. "There's a control panel for each of those small tanks. I choose the equation corresponding to each metal that we want and set it up on the panels. Six tanks, six equations. We'll choose magnesium, aluminum, copper, zinc, silver, and gold."

While Rick and his father watched, Doug turned dials and threw switches, setting up the equations on the board. Finally he turned to the scientist. He was smiling, but Rick saw that he was nervous. This first full-scale operation meant a lot to Doug.

"Will you throw the electrode switches, sir?" he invited.

"Thank you, Douglas," Hartson Brant returned. "I'd be honored."

The scientist walked to a separate panel where six numbered, knife-type switches corresponded to each of the tanks. One by one he threw them.

"Something's happening," Scotty called.

The four men outside the door came running. Mrs. Brant and Barby left the colorful tube banks and joined the group at the tanks. Soon eleven heads were bent over the tanks, crowding for a look.

Rick watched carefully. Bubbles were rising from one electrode in each tank, but that was only simple electrolysis as the current broke the liquid down into hydrogen and oxygen. The minerals would show at the other electrodes.

It was the No. 3 tank that showed results first. It was hard to tell through the green liquid, but the electrode seemed thicker.

"Number 3 off," Doug called hoarsely.

Rick jumped to the switch.

The young engineer lifted the electrode out, held it over a glass dish, and scraped with a thin, wooden blade. Wet, powdery metal fell in a little silver shower to the waiting glass. Doug looked at the interested faces around him.

"Pure aluminum," he said simply.

One by one the rest of the tanks built up their coatings of metals on the electrodes. Aluminum had come first, because there was a higher percentage of it in the residue liquid. Gold would come last, because there was less of it than the other metals.

But at last Doug called, "Number 6 off!" As he lifted the electrode, wet, yellow powder gleamed in the light!

Then they were all laughing and talking at once, and crowding around Doug with their congratulations.

The flustered, happy, young engineer laughingly pulled free. "Now," he said, "I propose that we eat!"

An outdoor table had been set up next to the Quonset hut and the delicious sea food dinner that Cap'n Galt, as caterer, had prepared, was waiting.

Much later, Rick pushed his chair back. He was filled to bursting with clam chowder and broiled lobster. A moment later, Scotty, the last one to finish, pushed his chair back, too, and beamed at the assembled company.

Tom Blakely requested: "Now, Mike, how about that report you promised us after dinner?"

"All right," Mike agreed. He rose and addressed them. "Some of you know most of what I have to say. It has been in the papers. But I have something new to add, from a talk I had with the district attorney. He expects Wessel to be sentenced to twenty years for attempted murder. Then he'll be tried on that old charge left over from the Spindrift Island moon rocket. He'll get about ten more for that. Tony probably will get twenty years, and Cunner ten. The Coast Guard found traces of the oyster poison on his boat, so that charge is waiting for Cunner, too. The poison was copper sulphate, by the way."

The private detective paused. "I'm sorry to announce that Brink will get only about five years in prison on the charge of harboring a criminal. However, the Department of Justice has taken an active interest. Their preliminary investigations into Brink's foreign tie-ups indicate that they'll find plenty more. It's even possible, one of their agents informed me by phone today, that they'll find enough evidence for a charge of treason. So I don't think we need worry any more about friend Brink." He looked at Rick. "And Jenkins had his phone disconnected because his health forced him out of business. So that teaches all young detectives not to jump to conclusions."

"I want to thank you all for coming," Doug said quietly as Mike finished. "It's an important day for Tom and me, and for Rick and Scotty, because we consider them partners, too. Tom and I are agreed that the boys should have a share in the plant, because without their help, we might never have brought our enemies to justice."

Rick and Scotty looked at each other, speechless. Then Rick jumped to his feet.

"Golly, Doug, we can't! I mean, we appreciate it, but we don't want any rewards!"

"I agree with Rick," Hartson Brant stated. "Besides, if they accepted even a small share in your plant, it would obligate them, in a sense. They would feel that they had to keep their jobs for the rest of the summer." He paused and looked at Rick, his eyes twinkling. "And we have other plans for them."

All thoughts of the sea mine plant vanished. Rick ran around to where his father was sitting, Scotty right behind him.

"A new experiment, Dad? What is it? Is it at Spindrift or somewhere else?"

"Not so fast." His father laughed. "We're not going to intrude on this celebration by talking about a new experiment. You'll just have to wait until we get home. Zircon and Weiss are arriving tomorrow."

Later, it was with some reluctance that the boys resigned their jobs at the plant, but already they were looking forward to a new adventure and speculating on what it might be.

Then, a few days later, they walked with Hartson Brant into the big laboratory on Spindrift Island and were greeted by Professor Zircon and Professor Weiss.

Zircon was perspiring over what looked like a huge brass ball. He looked up as they entered and growled, "Well, it's about time! One more day of this loafing up in Connecticut and we'd have left you home!"

But Rick and Scotty returned the big scientist's greeting absently, because their eyes were on an object in the center of the lab.

It was set in a steel cradle, and at first glance it looked like a dirigible, although much smaller. It had square, heavy quartz windows, and small propellers projected from the stern and from the sides. The nose was covered with strange devices.

As they stared, openmouthed, a door in the side opened and Julius Weiss crawled out.

"Don't stand there with your faces open," he snapped. "Get into lab smocks! We have a lot to do and only a short time to do it in."

Rick knew that the gruff greetings were the two scientists' way of letting the boys know that it was nice to have them back. He grinned and turned to his father.

"Dad, please tell us! We'll pop if you don't."

"Like a couple of melons," Scotty added. "I can feel my shirt buttons popping already."

"All right." Hartson Brant laughed. "Professor Gordon is waiting for us in Hawaii. He has chartered a suitable boat of some kind. I've also wired Chahda to come home and join us. He'll be here tomorrow. Then we'll all take a little trip."

"But where?" Rick pleaded.

"And what's that for?" Scotty asked.

"The trip," Hartson Brant said, "is to the island of Kwangara in the Western Pacific. And that object into which Weiss just crawled like a hermit crab is the Submobile, his own adaptation of the bathysphere. We must complete work on it in two weeks, so it can be shipped to Hawaii. Professor Gordon is working there with officials of the Bishop Museum, looking up all possible data on Alta-Yuan."

He smiled at the two eager faces before him.

"Alta-Yuan," he explained, "is a sunken temple. We're

going to explore it in an attempt to solve the mystery of the Pacific Polynesian migrations, a special assignment from the Pacific Ethnographic Society."

Rick turned his glance on the intriguing thing in the steel cradle.

"But why do we need that to explore a temple?"

"This temple," Hartson Brant said, "is one hundred fathoms down—at the bottom of the sea!"

RICK BRANT continues his exciting adventures in the next volume, **100 FATHOMS UNDER**. Don't miss this thrilling story of a treasure hunt by Submobile in the depths of the Pacific Ocean.

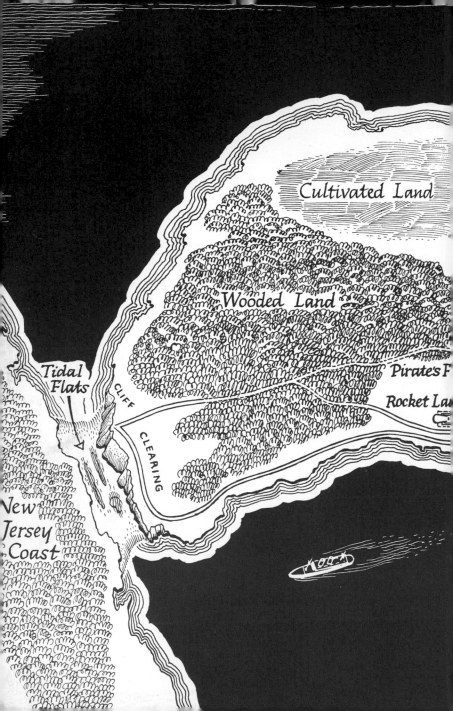